TALES FROM CHARLETON HOUSE

CHARLETON HOUSE MYSTERY SHORTS

KATE P ADAMS

April '22

Suzanne,
Thank you for your support.
Happy reading

Best wishes
Kate

ALSO BY KATE P ADAMS

Death by Dark Roast

A Killer Wedding

Sleep Like the Dead

A Deadly Ride

Mulled Wine and Murder

A Tragic Act

A Capital Crime

Tales from Charleton House

CONTENTS

A STYLISH REVENGE

*S*ophie was overwhelmed by the vast selection of sofas in front of her. All she really cared about was whether or not they were comfortable enough to fall asleep on after a long day at work. If they looked okay in her house, all the better. Okay would do.

But Joyce was concerned about aesthetics, curves, fabrics, and an atmosphere of calm that reflected both the neutrality of Sophie's sitting room (Joyce speak for 'boring white walls') and a little of Sophie's personality. Sophie wondered what would best reflect someone who spent most of her life covered in cat hair, ate cake for breakfast, drank too much gin and whose veins ran with coffee. At the moment, Joyce seemed to think that a modern emerald-green piece that was all sharp edges and looked horrendously uncomfortable fitted the bill perfectly, but this was Joyce's fifth interpretation of Sophie's personality in the last hour.

Joyce had been promising to take Sophie furniture shopping for two years. Sophie had always felt this was more of a threat than a promise, but she had run out of excuses, so here they were in one of Manchester's most exclusive furniture stores on a wet Wednesday afternoon. Sophie was concerned for the health of her bank balance as she looked at the price tags. Joyce, on the other hand, appeared perfectly at home in her knee-length orange designer coat, which looked as expensive as the furniture she was perusing. Her jet-black accessories did nothing to tone down the shocking vision she made as she strutted around the immense space, looking to all intents and purposes like the lady of the manor with limitless credit cards and a stately home to fill with expensive furniture. Sophie felt frumpy and a little awkward in comparison.

'Now then, I think this would look stunning underneath the window. If you renovated the fireplace, added some nice navy coloured tiles to the hearth, then this would really sing.' They were looking at a mustard-yellow Chesterfield, a Victorian style that Sophie rather liked, but the colour was pushing at the limits of her interior-design risk taking.

'I'm only after a sofa at this stage, I don't want to have to do anything else. It took me over two years to get this far; can you imagine how long it would take me to choose tiles, and then get round to actually fitting them? The sofa would need replacing by then.'

Joyce gave her a look of exasperation. 'True. Don't think I don't know you tried to get out of *this* shopping trip as well, my girl. Baking emergency, my bum. What a *ridiculous* idea.'

'Mark told you?'

'He might think that I'm Derbyshire's answer to Medusa, but he knows which side his bread is buttered. Yes, he told me. Now, what about that one?' As Joyce swept off between a line of ottomans and coffee tables, Sophie plopped herself down on a vivid red loveseat. She was surprised that Joyce hadn't suggested it – it was only a couple of shades lighter than her friend's lipstick. Watching as the older woman ummed and ahhed over a large modular set, Sophie knew she would be told when Joyce had made her decision, having completely forgotten that the sofa wasn't actually for her.

Just don't let it be animal print, Sophie said to herself. *Please don't let it be animal print.*

Her eyes drifted across the room to a large squishy-looking three-seater covered in a lurid animal print in shades of pink. Sophie couldn't think of a time or place when something like that could be considered appropriate, unless this was where Derbyshire's brothel owners came for furniture.

Sophie watched her friend, who had moved on. Clearly distracted by something, Joyce was paying little attention to the rather nice dusky blue sofa and armchair in front of her. Sophie followed Joyce's eye line, unsurprised to find her watching a rather smartly dressed and handsome older man as he examined a simple cream armchair. Joyce had long been searching for her Prince Charming, an ambition that had not been dimmed in the slightest by at least four ex-husbands (Sophie wasn't entirely sure of the exact number).

The object of Joyce's attention was just shy of six feet tall. Neatly trimmed silver-grey hair, short but not too short, was discreetly styled at the front with no excessive use of hair products. He appeared to be in his late sixties and wore a navy-blue pinstriped suit, a purple tie and pink shirt. Sophie imagined him smelling of a particularly attractive and expensive aftershave.

Perhaps a delicate musk, she thought.

He occasionally rested his hand on the arm of an attractive and clearly much younger blonde woman, who looked up at him adoringly every time she felt his touch.

'I reckon you can take her. He'll be yours in minutes,' Sophie said to her friend as Joyce joined her.

'No thanks, damaged goods,' she replied, but her eyes never once left the man's face as she spoke.

'Really? I would have thought he's just your type.'

'He is – I mean, *was* my type. That, dear girl, is ex-husband number three.'

The surprise registered immediately on Sophie's face and she regretted not being more guarded.

'What, too good for me?' Joyce asked with mock offence. 'Surprised I could get my claws into a suave surgeon?'

'You mean like a cosme...'

'No, I do not mean like a cosmetic surgeon. What are you suggesting? Every part of me is in its original perfect condition. Surgeon as in orthopaedics. It turns out there's a lot of money in knees – it's thanks to him and his extracurricular activities that I have the house. You don't think I could afford a five-bedroom detached on my salary, do you?'

Sophie had no idea. She'd never visited Joyce's home.

'*Extracurricular* activities?'

'I kicked him out for playing away from home. After which, he went on to marry his own number three, Barbara. And that woman clinging on to his arm over there, barely out of her teens, is *not* wife number three. I vaguely know Barbara, and I know for a fact they're still together – they both attended a benefit last month. It was in one of those local lifestyle magazines, there was a picture of them shaking hands with the mayor. I'd bet my entire shoe collection that is his latest bit of fluff and his wife has been, like me, taken for a fool.'

Her shoe collection? Had Joyce really just staked her shoe collection? Sophie knew she was serious.

'Are you going to talk to him?'

'Why would I do that? No, I'm going to let him and his little dolly bird enjoy their outing undisturbed.'

Joyce strutted off and Sophie quickly followed on behind.

'I'm still thinking that emerald green one would make a nice statement. It would be very easy for you to add some accent pieces, and that fat cat of yours would look good on it. Pumpkin's tabby browns would go nicely with the green backdrop.' Now even Pumpkin was an accessory to be taken into account.

Sophie wasn't so sure. The sofa was a stunning colour and a

part of her was clapping and cheering at the idea of something so bold, but in practice it was still a step too far for her. She would need to work her way up to something so daring.

'You know, I'm rather hoping that if I can get you to up your game with your furniture, you'll let me work on your wardrobe. That still needs a little improvement.' Sophie wasn't offended. She'd heard this sort of comment so often that it had lost its sting, plus she knew Joyce was right. In fact, by 'a little', Joyce was being kind.

'I've worn a few bright scarves that you've approved of.'

'Yes, I'll give you that, but it's not enough. Not nearly…'

'Joyce.' The handsome surgeon had interrupted them, standing close enough to Sophie that she could smell his after-shave. And she'd been right: it was a mellow musk. She wanted to spend the rest of the day inhaling it.

'Edgar.' Joyce didn't look happy, but she held his eye and attempted to squeeze what vaguely resembled a smile out of one side of her mouth.

'Ed, please.'

'Of course, I'd forgotten how much you dislike to be called Edgar. Feel it ages you, don't you?'

He smiled, looking aware that he wasn't going to win this one. 'You look very well,' he offered, sounding genuine.

'Yes, yes, I do, Edgar. You don't look too shabby yourself.' She glanced towards the young woman who was looking at a display of candelabras and flicking quick looks in their direction. 'So, how is Barbara?'

'She's very well, visiting her mother this week.'

'You're not going to introduce me to your *young* friend?'

'Sally? She's just started working in the administration team at the clinic, offered to help me pick out some new furniture for the waiting room.'

Sophie was watching him intently. He wasn't in the slightest bit nervous. If Joyce was right, then Edgar was not at all concerned that she had caught him out. It seemed that he knew that Joyce knew and she knew that he knew she knew, which put Sophie's brain in a momentary knot.

He was the smooth, confident kind of character that Sophie found it easy to imagine Joyce with. It would require a very self-assured man to take on a woman often referred to by her staff as the Dragon Lady, or by their mutual friend Mark as Cruella de Vil. Edgar certainly came across as the man for that job, but it appeared that he had got a little overconfident and decided to take the risk of having more than one woman in his life – quite a big risk when one of those women was Joyce Brocklehurst. She would be more than enough for the average bloke.

The whole scene was looking more and more like some sort of middle-class, furniture-based stand-off. Sophie wasn't sure what might happen next, until Sally came to the rescue.

'Sorry, Ed, I don't mean to disturb you, but we need to be back at the office in half an hour.' She smiled sweetly, a blank look in her eyes showing she had absolutely no idea who Edgar was talking to.

'Of course, on my way. Joyce, lovely to see you.' He smiled at Sophie before heading towards a young male sales assistant who looked poised to take an order. Joyce watched with a far-off look in her eyes.

'If I know anything about him, that furniture isn't going anywhere near the clinic. He's up to his old tricks.'

'Meaning?'

'She's not just staff, she's his type for a bit on the side. She's almost a carbon copy of the woman he was fooling around with when I kicked him out. One of the reasons I knew what he was up to was because, with the use of some sleuthing skills not unlike the ones you have displayed since you joined our merry band of staff up at Charleton House, I discovered he had just rented a little flat in the city centre. A love nest, if you will; or lust nest, more like. I'd put money on him doing the same thing again and Barbara being nowhere near her mother's. She's at home, blissfully unaware. Or perhaps she's aware that something is not quite right, she just doesn't know what yet.'

As she spoke, Joyce moved her eyes to the sales assistant who had walked Edgar and Sally over to a computer and was imputing details. Edgar's credit card was already in his hand.

'I bet that's for his business account. A lust nest that is fully tax deductible.' After another couple of seconds, Joyce turned to Sophie. 'Right! Enough of that. We're here for you. Let's find you the sofa of your dreams, then go and get a drink.'

Joyce had a determined look that left Sophie feeling a little nervous. Unsure if she was now more or less likely to end up with something that would terrify Pumpkin and give her nightmares, Sophie took a deep breath and followed behind Joyce, who could walk at a remarkable pace despite skyscraper-high heels.

For the next half hour, Sophie was regaled with the benefits of leather, cross weave, chenille or velvet; of the two-seater over the three-seater; how long the sofa needed to be if Sophie was to comfortably sleep on it (6 inches longer than she was tall, which would rule out having friends sleep on it; Sophie was a mere 5 foot).

'How do you know all this stuff? Or more importantly, why do you know all this?'

'I enjoy design as much as some people enjoy looking at 200-year-old paintings in ugly gold frames. I could tell you everything you need to know about Le Corbusier or Eames. I also know a few things about the work of Chippendale and Hepplewhite, although I'd never have any of their work in my house, it's not to my taste.'

Not enough animal print, Sophie thought, simultaneously amazed that Joyce was referencing a Chippendale that wasn't clad in a G-string.

'Take this one, for example.' Joyce walked over to a rather

boxy sofa with high sides. It was covered in a pale grey velvet, a delicate pattern swirling across the fabric. 'The Knole Sofa. A direct descendant of one created in the 1630s and now found at Knole House in Kent. It was a sort of double throne and used as a chair of state.' She gave Sophie a knowing look. 'Not just a pretty face.'

Before Sophie could respond, Joyce's head spun and she gave a hoot of triumph. 'Now this! This is it! This is the one, Sophie, I've found it. Not too feminine – I know you won't want that – but with the right accessories – cushions, a new rug – this would look just heavenly. I need a sales assistant. Excuse me...'

Sophie looked at what was about to become her new sofa, her 'signature piece', and smiled. Joyce had indeed done it, Sophie needn't have worried. There was more to Joyce than lipstick and nail polish; she knew her stuff.

Once the sofa had been paid for and delivery arranged, Joyce led Sophie to a bar around the corner from the shop for a glass of sparkling wine. As Joyce ordered the drinks, Sophie admired the photo of the sofa she had taken with her phone. A vintage espresso-brown tufted leather piece with buttons, it had, according to Joyce, beautifully tooled legs and finely crafted miniature brass wheels. On its own, you'd assume that it would look right at home in a dark library surrounded by first-edition copies of Dickens or Austen, but Joyce had convinced her that with an array of accessories, it would be perfect.

Sophie had left the shop with armfuls of cushions in a variety of creams and beiges, a sheepskin rug, which would be a devil to keep clean with Pumpkin around, and a collection of designer cream candles. Sophie's end-terrace worker's cottage was going to have a rustic look; it would be serious and moody, but also luxurious with a classic style.

'Just keep everything around it light and airy,' Joyce had instructed her.

The sofa and all the trimmings had cost Sophie a month's salary, give or take, but she was excited. This was the first thing she had done to really make the house hers, to put her mark on it (if you discounted the vintage hand-crank coffee grinder and the extortionately priced bright-red fridge-freezer, now doubling as a cat perch, in the kitchen, both of which she adored and had moved into the house before anything else had crossed the threshold).

'Are you pleased?' asked Joyce, taking a sip and wincing at the taste of the wine. 'This is awful.'

'Very, I love it. The sofa, I mean, not the wine.'

'I know you thought I'd be forcing some godforsaken luminous sequin-covered mash of rainbow colours onto you. Do you have a little more faith in me now?'

'I do.' Sophie looked sheepish. Joyce's description of her expectations was spot on.

Joyce kept sipping at her glass, despite her disdain for its contents. She seemed distracted, deep in thought. Sophie wasn't used to her being this quiet.

'You okay?'

'Hmm, just thinking. What do you make of this wine?'

'Not the best I've had.'

'Good, get it down you. I have an idea.' Joyce stood up and tipped back what was left of the wine in one swift movement. 'Come on. Waste not, want not.' Sophie mirrored her friend, narrowly avoiding choking on the vinegary fizz. Then they marched out of the wine bar and back towards the furniture store.

Joyce scanned the room.

'Right, where is he? Looked barely old enough to tie his own shoelaces. There he is. Okay, I need you to keep your distance; I have to look like I'm here on my own. Hopefully he won't recognise me from earlier.'

Sophie nodded, although if the young assistant had spotted Joyce, it was unlikely he wouldn't remember her. Sophie's friend was not the kind of woman anyone forgot, but Joyce was on a mission and she had no intention of getting in the way of her plans.

As Joyce marched up to the young sales assistant, who was tapping away on a keyboard, Sophie positioned herself within hearing distance and pretended to be admiring a pale yellow love seat. Joyce slowed down as she approached, smiled, softened her posture and went from a ramrod-straight missile to a slightly more approachable, demure figure, resting a hand on the counter.

'Hello…' she examined his badge, 'Tom. Oh wonderful, my boss told me it was a young man by the name of Tom who assisted him earlier. I do hope that's you.' She smiled again, Sophie assumed in her best attempt at 'sweetly'.

'Erm, maybe. What's his name? What did he look like?'

'Edgar Braun. Pinstripe suit, pink shirt, purple tie, silver hair. He had a blonde lady with him.'

'I remember, they bought one of the Hayes Glamour Maxi four-seaters. Is there a problem?'

'Yes, although not with your service. He was saying how efficient and helpful you were. It's just that he got back to the office and decided that he might have rather pushed his wife towards the sofa that was really his choice, and now he feels extremely guilty. He was wondering if there was any way that he could change the order, or is it too late?' A pained expression crossed her face.

'I'm sure I can do that; which sofa did he want to go with?'

Joyce scanned the room, her eyes narrowing as she set her

sights on her prey. 'That one matches the description he gave me perfectly.'

Tom looked taken aback. 'Wow, that is different.'

'You can see why my boss feels guilty now. He really did go for his taste, not his wife's. He wants to make her happy, but got carried away when he saw the Hayes model.'

'Okay, only this one is a little less expensive so there'll be a refund.'

'Fabulous, so we can add the matching ottoman?'

Tom did a quick calculation. 'If you take both the sofa and the ottoman, the price is exactly the same as for the Hayes Glamour. I can make a swap on the order.'

'Wonderful, Tom, you are a star. There is just one other thing.' Tom looked at her expectantly. 'Once he got back to the office, he realised he'd asked you to send the bill to his clinic. That would be fine, only his wife manages their finances and it would be best if you could send it to their home address. Make sure it is addressed to Barbara Braun. Is that okay?'

'Of course, let me jot that down.'

Joyce rattled off an address from memory. 'Could you also make sure the delivery address is on the invoice for their records? Knowing him, he gave you the address for the clinic for that, too.' This was followed by another of Joyce's interpretations of a sweet smile.

'Flat 22, Park View.'

Sophie knew exactly where that was. A converted brewery, the flats were the height of modern living. Quite a fancy love nest.

'Phew, that's right. If he's not had his morning quota of coffee, he can get a little forgetful. Tom, you have been an absolute sweetheart and you have made my day considerably less stressful. You'll be management in no time at all, I'm sure of it.'

Even from a discreet distance, Sophie could have sworn that she saw Tom blush. To add to the poor boy's embarrassment,

Joyce reached across the counter and gave his arm a squeeze. With another smile, she turned and strode out of the store.

Before leaving, Sophie went to take a closer look at the sofa that would now be arriving at Edgar's love nest, and for which his wife would be receiving a fully itemised bill. She stood before the bright-pink, animal-print three-seater that had caught her eye earlier. The matching ottoman was pink-and-grey faux (she hoped) snakeskin. It would be visible from the moon; thank God she hadn't annoyed Joyce in the run-up to this trip, otherwise it might have been delivered to her house.

Her final thought as she left to catch up with Joyce was that she'd love to be a fly on the wall the day that Barbara opened the envelope containing the bill. It seemed that for Joyce, revenge was a dish best eaten while sitting on a bright-pink, animal-print sofa.

MEET THE FAMILY

*J*oe took a deep breath and opened the front door. Tightening his grip on Ellie's hand, he led her into his parents' house.

'We're here,' he called out. 'You ready for this?' he asked his girlfriend quietly. 'We can always turn and run, there's still time.'

Ellie smiled, squeezed his hand and pulled him down the corridor.

'You're a police officer, for heaven's sake, you've dealt with worse than this.'

'Have I?' he asked, pulling a face.

'I'm the one who should be nervous, not you. Worried they won't like me?'

'They'll love you. But you should be prepared...'

'You made it! Did you get lost?' shouted Gary, Joe's father, as they walked into a large airy kitchen. Wrapping Joe in a hug, he slapped him firmly on the back. Gary was a tall, broad-shouldered man with long grey hair. His bare feet, torn jeans and Hawaiian shirt gave him the look of a retired surfer. 'Ellie, love, good to finally meet you.' She received an equally enveloping hug and grinned at Joe over the shoulder crushed against her face. An old yellow Labrador rubbed against her leg before returning to a sofa and closing its eyes.

'This is my mum, Helen.'

A woman with maroon hair that shot out from her head in giant spirals kissed both of Ellie's cheeks, and then looked back at her son.

'This must be serious, you've ironed your shirt.'

Joe hesitated. 'Actually, Ellie did it.'

'OK, so at least you combed your hair.'

Ellie giggled. 'He used my hairbrush before we got out of the car.'

'Well, I guess you know what you've let yourself in for. Right, wine? Gin and tonic?'

Helen waved her glass in the air and Ellie replied, 'Wine, thanks. I'll open it. Where do you keep your corkscrew?'

'I like her,' Helen said to Joe as she passed Ellie a corkscrew in the shape of a parrot.

Gary had prepared a roast dinner fit for the gods. Slices of tender beef lay next to perfectly crispy potatoes, carrots and parsnips, all dotted with a sprinkling of chopped rosemary. Broad beans and peas that had come from the garden dripped with butter. Two fat Yorkshire puddings the size of saucers balanced precariously on top of each plate of food. The gravy was the perfect consistency, thick but not too thick, and the bread sauce creamy.

'Not sure you're meant to serve bread sauce with beef, but I ain't serving a Sunday roast without it,' explained Gary as he set the plates on the table. 'Tuck in, folks, don't be shy.'

The beef melted in Ellie's mouth, the outer crisp of the potatoes giving way to a smoothly delicious inside. Gary grinned at her as she added a dollop of bread sauce.

'Not bad, eh?'

'It's fantastic, thank you. Do you cook, Helen?'

Her question was followed by a guffaw from Gary. 'I love my wife madly, but she can burn water.'

'He's right.' Helen leant against her husband playfully. 'It's why I married him. I'd starve otherwise.'

Helen's gin and tonic appeared to be the glassware equivalent of Mary Poppins's carpet bag: utterly bottomless. Ellie watched her take another slug, remembering that Joe had told her how his mum liked a drink. However, he wasn't worried; she could also go for months without touching a drop. She simply enjoyed a good time when the moment struck her.

Helen's tiny waist sat atop thin legs which propelled her around the room in a single constant motion, revealing her long-past dancing career. Ellie found her captivating. Joe, like his father, was softer, both in appearance and manner.

Ellie took in the room as they ate and chatted. A well-preserved dark wooden Art Deco sideboard dominated one wall of the dining room, its clear lines and sharp patterns looking at home in the bright open-plan space and alongside the sleek modern furniture in primary colours. The different styles each drew attention to the richness of the other.

'That looks like an Epstein,' Ellie said, both intrigued by the sideboard and seeking a way to change the subject. Helen was regaling them with far too much information regarding her recent colonic irrigation.

'Well spotted, although it's a copy. It was my aunt's. She died a couple of months ago. The front room is full of her furniture; I can hardly get in for the stuff. Can't quite bring myself to get rid of it all yet.'

'I'm sorry,' said Ellie, looking at Joe and wondering why he hadn't told her there had been a death in the family.

'Wonderful woman, our Aunt Mildred, wasn't she, Gary?' Helen continued and her husband nodded, clearly aware that an actual response was not required. 'Beautiful too; you should have seen her. In fact, I'll show you.'

Still nibbling on a piece of Yorkshire pudding, which she picked up in her fingers and took with her, Helen left the room. Joe and Gary grinned at one another.

'Joe!' Ellie was confused. 'You should have said you'd lost...'

'I only met her once, I think, when I was about four. She was hardly a close relative.'

'No, but after a gin and tonic, she takes on a mythical status,' Gary added. 'From what I've heard, she could light up a room by movin' away from the window.'

'What was that, Gary?' Helen lurched back into the room carrying a large painting.

'Just sayin' what a lovely woman Mildred was. She joining us for dessert?'

Helen placed a portrait on the sideboard and made sure it was leaning securely against the wall. It showed an attractive woman, somewhere in her fifties, her hair neatly styled in gentle waves. Her curious eyes looked out across the room. It was hard to separate her shoulders from the background; there was an eerie floating quality that put Ellie slightly on edge. At least Helen hadn't propped the picture up on a chair and had Mildred join them for dinner at the table itself.

As the meal went on, Helen's words slurred a little, but she remained steady and coherent.

'She would have loved to have been here, to have met you, Ellie. She would have thought you were marvellous – so pretty, so clever. Just marvellous, really marvellous. She should be here, you know.' Ellie caught Gary raising an eyebrow at his son. 'I'll get her, she should join us.'

Helen stood up and left the room a second time. 'Gary,' she called from the other side of the door, 'will you get the coffee on?'

He stood, looked at them both and, shaking his head, said, 'I have no idea,' before walking to the open-plan kitchen behind them.

'Thank you,' said Joe, giving Ellie a quick kiss on the cheek.

'What for?'

'Your apparently endless patience. I'll understand if this is our last date.' The look on his face was one of amusement, with tiny amounts of hope and fear mixed in around the edges.

Ellie laughed. 'Your mother is brilliant. A little, well…'

'…drunk?'

'I was going to say unusual.'

Joe laughed. 'I can't disagree.'

'Here we are.' Gary put a tray of coffee cups and a French press on the table. 'Come on, Helen, coffee's ready.'

Helen reappeared and threw herself back into her seat, both hands clutching a small squat pot.

'Sorry, sorry, took a while to find Mildred. Wonderful, coffee; will you be mother, Gary? Now, this is Mildred.'

Helen placed the pot on the table. It was a rich brown colour with a wide black band painted around the lower half. She lifted the lid and stared inside.

'Hello, Mildred.' She looked up. 'You should all say hello.' With the lid still on the table beside her, Helen handed the pot to Joe, who responded by looking imploringly across the table at his father. Gary shrugged and continued to lay out the coffee cups.

'Umm, hello, Mildred,' said Joe, handing the pot to Ellie with an extremely apologetic expression on his face. Ellie stared into the darkness. Inside was a fine pale-grey powder.

Mildred's ashes had just joined them for coffee. Ellie was holding an urn. She wasn't sure where to look, let alone what to do or say. They were quite literally saying hello to Aunt Mildred.

Ellie looked up at her date, who echoed his father's shrug, his eyebrows raised in another apology.

'OK, well, hello, Mildred. Very nice to meet you.' Ellie passed the urn on to Gary, relieved to get rid of Aunt Mildred.

''Ello, Mildred. You're looking well. Hope you don't mind, but we're using your fruit dish as a water bowl for the dog.' He placed the urn back in front of his wife. 'Don't knock her over, I don't want to have to hoover her up. We'll never be able to separate her from the dog hair.'

The silence that followed was broken only by the sound of the coffee plunger and the filling of mugs. The milk jug was passed around, and then the sugar bowl. Ellie handed the sugar to Helen, who added two teaspoons to her cup, stirring them in slowly.

'Mildred liked sugar in her coffee, and tea, three big spoonfuls.' She reached for a clean spoon and scooped out some of Mildred's ashes. 'I wonder what it would be like if I added her to my coffee.' She looked genuinely fascinated.

'Alright, dear,' said Gary, firm and commanding as he quickly reached for the spoon. 'I think we've had enough of this for tonight, haven't we.' There was still a gentleness to him; no annoyance crept out between his words and he looked at his wife with affection after he'd returned some indeterminate part of Aunt Mildred to the safety of her urn. With the lid firmly back in place, Mildred was put on the dresser in front of her portrait, which had a look of bewildered amusement that Ellie hadn't spotted before.

'Don't worry,' Gary was looking at Ellie and Joe, 'I'll get the superglue out in the morning. *You* are a very welcome guest, Ellie, but I don't plan on having Mildred round for dinner again any time soon.'

Ellie glanced over at Joe, who looked back with an expression of mild horror. She knew he'd be feeling deeply embarrassed and reached under the table to give his leg a squeeze.

They say people turn into their parents, thought Ellie. *If this is a sign of the future, then I'm just going to have to make sure that all our relatives end up in an urn with a lid I can lock. I'm also going to make sure I watch my coffee being made. Better still, I hereby commit to always being the one who makes the coffee in our house.*

A LASTING MARK

*H*arriet Smedley had been a self-appointed guardian of the Charleton House chapel for as long as anyone could remember. A regular worshipper since childhood, she'd made the chapel a second home, a place of solace in a crazy world that she increasingly felt was not deserving of her time and attention. She would guard it with ferocity until she made her final visit in a wooden box.

The chapel was set deep within the grounds of Charleton House, the ancestral home of the Fitzwilliam-Scott family, and an architectural jewel in the rolling hills of Derbyshire. A glorious building, with its alabaster altar and stained-glass windows, pews made of wood taken from trees on the Charleton estate, it was watched over by gilded angels. The visitors and their behaviour, on the other hand, were watched over by Harriet. Her official role as a chapel volunteer gave her an opportunity to have an impact on its day-to-day running, and her stern reputation – something she was well aware of – ensured that people followed the rules when she was around.

As she patrolled the space, her footsteps echoed off the stone floor. Her movements were quick and fluid; after all, she knew the chapel so well, she could find her way around it in the dark, which had been useful in more than one power cut. Her eyes were just as quick, darting around, watching everyone who came in. Did that small child have sticky fingers? What might he touch? Was that woman's rucksack going to knock into things? That man checking his phone – rude enough in itself, but was he also about to take a prohibited photograph? Was that a member of staff who had walked in with a cup of coffee? Food and drink were not permitted in the chapel, and they really ought to know better.

But for all her external hardness, Harriet had a softer side, and contrary to popular opinion, a caring heart did beat within her slim frame. She had attended every wedding, whether or not she knew the bride or groom, and watched the exchange of vows with a tear in her eye. She paid her respects at every funeral, and brought to every baptism a hope for a long and happy life.

She had her own ideas on how the chapel should be run, of course, and knew that it would be for the best if her suggestions were put in place. Harriet made sure she knew the chapel diary off by heart; not even a lightbulb could be changed without her knowledge, so it was with some concern that she had watched a small group of Charleton House staff arrive and settle around a pew at the back, notebooks in hand. She recognised the three people as James, a curator, Ellie, a member of the conservation team, and Abigail, a project manager.

Harriet was always suspicious when these departments came together. Collaboration between their staff could result in some beautiful restoration work or an exhibition that threw new light onto the Duke and Duchess's magnificent art collection, both of which Harriet thoroughly approved of. However, their endeavours had also resulted in some more questionable 'modern' work: Harriet particularly remembered a special scratch-and-sniff map which visitors used to experience the smells that would have inhabited the house in centuries past. In one room, a little box on the map issued the aroma of logs burning in an enormous fire-place; in the dining room, a scratch resulted in a whiff of cooked meat. Harriet had resisted sniffing the foul aroma of a water closet or Georgian toilet; that had taken the already ridiculous idea too far.

Now she watched nervously as James and Ellie examined marks on the narrow shelf at the back of the pew, while Abigail made notes. A cluster of initials had been carved into the wood over the decades, and although Harriet abhorred graffiti of all kinds, she also understood that time and history changed the environment, and what we might call graffiti now would actually tell fascinating stories to future generations about those who came before. She was as protective of those stories as she was the tiles on the floor, the kneeling cushions, or the pipes of the organ. These simple childlike scratches were part of the fabric of the chapel; the fingers that had run across them over the years had left behind a wonderfully smooth, soft feel to the wood that she enjoyed as she walked past and reached out to touch them. They were here and they should stay, although she would of course ensure that there were no additions carved by bored school-children, or others with more criminal intent.

Harriet fully understood the historical value of ancient graffiti. In the Tower of London, where Philip Howard, Earl of Arundel, was imprisoned by Elizabeth I before being sentenced to death in 1589, he had carved his name into the walls along with the words:

'The more affliction we endure for Christ in this world, the more glory we shall get with Christ in the world to come.'

Conservation works at Hampton Court Palace, once the home of Henry VIII, had revealed graffiti, presumably left by bored workmen in the 1730s. There is the outline of a pair of shoes and the beginning of a dress. Harriet had been fortunate to go on a rare tour into the attics at Kew Palace, famous as the residence of George III, where she had been shown the 'witch marks' carved into the beams. They had presumably been left by carpenters when the palace was being built and were believed to ward off evil spirits.

However the interest of the Charleton House staff, in a meeting she had been unaware of, made her uneasy. Harriet took it upon herself to monitor the activity of the group; the nature of their jobs did not, in her opinion, preclude them from making an avoidable mistake. It was with great annoyance, and just a little satisfaction at how right she had been about this, that she noticed James had left a trail of dried mud, clumps of which had fallen from his trainers.

'Trainers, of all things,' she muttered. Charleton House, a place of such beauty and importance, deserved a pair of proper well-polished leather shoes, like those worn by the tour guide Mark Boxer. The man was a little over-pleased with his own skills and knowledge, but it had to be said, he made an effort with his appearance.

Harriet appeared behind the group with a dustpan and brush.

'Was that me?' James asked, peering through his round tortoiseshell glasses. 'Oops.'

Oops, Harriet repeated to herself as she walked away to discard the mud. No apology, no look of shame, just *oops*. *He may well have a PhD*, she mused, *but common sense and good manners are another thing entirely.*

A visitor caught her eye as she returned. 'No food in the chapel,' she stated firmly at a middle-aged woman with fake eyelashes so thick and heavy looking that Harriet was surprised she could open her eyes at all.

'No problem, it's chewing gum,' the woman explained with a smile.

'It is a problem if it goes in your mouth with the intention of being chewed or swallowed,' Harriet clarified and offered up a small bin. The woman, with some reluctance and a look of disdain, slowly dropped the lump of gum into it.

With her usual swiftness, Harriet returned to the meeting. The pew which was holding the focus of their attention was furthest away from any natural light in a gloomy section of the chapel, so it was no surprise that people had been able to leave their mark in the wood without being spotted. Harriet drew a little closer and peered through the gap between the gathered heads, listening intently to their conversation.

Her shoulders tensed. She wasn't prepared for this. There hadn't been any messages left in the vestry about upcoming work. Were they considering removing the pew? Had woodworm set in without her noticing? Had it been damaged by visitors? Had it been decided that the marks were unsightly and had no historic value? The idea that something had slipped past her caused a tightness in her stomach.

'WL is Lord William Longley,' James was telling the group. 'He was probably about fourteen years old when he did this, and he was caught by his mother who was particularly mortified as they were guests of the Duke and Duchess in the late 1800s.'

Correct, Harriet thought, *everyone knows that.*

'This one, WP, tucked away down the side, is most likely William Polt, one of the carpenters who did some repair work in 1927. A stonemason who was here at the same time has left his own marks on the walls of the staircase that leads down to the basement.'

'And these?' Harriet leaned over to get a closer look at the set of initials Abigail was pointing at.

'This one,' James grinned, 'is our own Duke. He admitted to it over a glass of wine a couple of months ago.'

Harriet looked at the carefully etched lines of the letters AFS. It had long been assumed that the current Duke, Alexander Fitzwilliam-Scott, had been responsible, but when quizzed about it, he would only ever reply with a little smile and the comment of 'Do you really think I would do such a thing?'

'This one we are less sure of.' James ran his finger along the two letters HA. 'We suspect it's possibly around 100 years old.'

Wrong, thought Harriet, wondering how this young man had ever achieved his doctorate.

'We have a strong suspicion that it might be Harrison Althrop, who visited a couple of times in 1919 and 1921 and was known for his high jinks. We know he did a similar thing at Shelden House, his uncle's home in Yorkshire. He was good friends with one of the current Duke's relatives.'

'Wrong again.'

'Sorry?' James turned to face Harriet, who silently cursed herself for speaking out loud. He smiled uncertainly, but was apparently keen to know what she had said. 'Do you know anything about this?'

'Of course not.'

The curator turned away from the notoriously grumpy volunteer and back to his colleagues.

One hundred? Harriet said, this time most definitely to herself. *You're only out by about fifty years.*

Harriet took a seat across the aisle, close enough to hear, far enough away to be ignored. If anything was going to happen to the marks on the pew shelf, she wanted to know about it. But after the conversation turned to lamination and low iron content, it no longer made much sense to Harriet and her attention drifted.

Two young men had entered the chapel, each with a young woman on his arm. All four of them carried motorcycle helmets, which Harriet paid particular attention to. It was well within the realms of possibility that at least one of those helmets was going to get bashed against the corner of a display case, or the edge of the 300-year-old font. It didn't go unnoticed by Harriet that both girls were wearing shorts, perfectly acceptable for the hot weather they were experiencing, but not at all suitable for riding on a motorbike. Then she gave herself a mild rebuke as she pictured herself as a nineteen-year-old on the back of a motor-bike in a pair of shorts. Back in the 1960s, it had not even been necessary to wear a helmet, but now Harriet was shocked at her own careless attitude to safety.

But it was different back then, she thought. *So little traffic on the roads, especially around here. The bikes were much slower, and anyway, I did take to covering up once my mother found out and insisted that I at least wear a decent pair of trousers.*

When Harriet had first heard that Eric had bought a motor-bike, she had been afraid for his safety. It had seemed so reckless. Of course, she now recognised that for a twenty-year-old, it was a natural thing for him to do, especially back then when he could never have afforded a car. All she could imagine at the time was that an accident was sure to follow.

But when Eric had first pulled up on the brand new shiny red bike, a smile plastered across his face which seemed to stretch quite literally from the base of one ear to the other, his thin blond hair sticking out in all sorts of crazy directions and the light that always seemed to shine in his bright blue eyes burning stronger than ever, all that she could think was that he belonged on it. It was as though he had found an extra part of himself that neither of them had known was missing.

He was – as hard as it was to imagine – even more handsome on the bike. Harriet had known that her mother would never approve, so when the day came that she finally agreed to climb on board and wrap her arms around Eric's waist, they had met at a friend's house, a mile away from her home, her mother, and the prying eyes of her neighbours. With no more to protect her than a pair of shorts and a t-shirt, she had swung her leg over the back of the bike and clung on to Eric tightly enough to sever him at the waist.

It had taken only minutes for Harriet to get over her fear and fully grasp why the bike had brought a smile to his face. She remembered its regal name, the Royal Enfield. He had been full of ideas about where they could go, and they had made many of them happen. Strapping a tent to the back of the bike and setting off in whichever direction the wind blew them, they had ridden to Scotland, a holiday that was spent mainly in the tent. Not for romantic reasons, but because the midges had viewed them as pieces of prime steak. They'd explored Wales in pouring rain, the enormous drops bouncing off the helmets they had by then taken to wearing, and Eric pulling up under every bridge to give them a moment of respite. Despite the challenges Mother Nature had thrown at them, they had loved every minute.

A few weeks after they had started riding together, they took a short run up to Charleton House. Eric had never seen the chapel and Harriet had wanted to share it with him. They had been courting for six months by now and he had become all that she could think about; she had even dared on occasion to wonder what a future with him might look like.

He had entered the chapel with what she viewed as a suitable amount of reverence and was vocal about just how beautiful it was. He too had been fascinated by the graffiti on the back pew, expressing his surprise but nodding his understanding as she explained that it was now part of the history of the place, part of the story of Charleton House.

'A story that you're part of too,' he had commented.

'Perhaps, but not a very important one.'

'The most important one, to me anyway.' He had smiled at her gently, and then continued to explore the chapel.

Harriet had walked down the aisle, giving herself a moment to reflect on what he had just said, wondering if he'd meant what she thought he meant, wondering if she would walk down this aisle under quite different circumstances. A few moments later, she turned to see him sitting in a pew at the back of the chapel.

He was preoccupied by something, but when he looked up and spotted her watching, he smiled sheepishly.

The following day, Harriet returned to help refresh the floral display and curiosity took her to where Eric had been sitting. And to her horror, she saw what he had done. Next to some well-worn marks, which had always been assumed to be the initials of wayward members of the Fitzwilliam-Scott family, was a freshly scratched set of initials: her own.

HA. Harriet Archibald.

When she had next seen Eric for a walk in the house gardens, he had tried to explain.

'I know it was a pretty unforgivable way of doing it, but you are part of the story of this house and that deserved to be captured. Others have done it, and you're important.'

'My name appears in chapel meeting minutes, that would have been enough. And anyway, God knows I'm here; he knows what I do.'

Eric had looked at the ground nervously before smiling and saying, 'I also wanted to capture you as you are now, Harriet Archibald, before your initials change.'

'Change? Why would they change? Oh... do you mean...?'

'Yes, Harriet Archibald, I'd like to change your initials to HS, if you'll have me.'

She hadn't needed to give his question any thought.

'Yes, Eric Smedley, I will.'

The following embrace had resulted in a chorus of whistles from a group of gardeners who were walking past.

In later years, Harriet would refer to his act of romantic vandalism and remind him that she had married a 'criminal', to which they would both laugh and he would call her his gangster's moll. After Eric had died a week shy of his fiftieth birthday, the initials he had carved in the wood had served as a comfort and Harriet returned to them time and time again, resting a hand over them, feeling him by her side.

. . .

Harriet tried to refocus on the conversation between the Charleton House staff. More dried mud had fallen off James's trainers, but she was distracted by their discussion.

'How would we secure it?'

'We'll find a way to wrap it or pressure fix it; we don't want to drill any holes in the wood. We can then add some information and we'd record a small piece to add to the audio tour.'

'You'll be securing what to the pew?' Harriet asked with urgency, having fully returned from her thoughts. The group all looked surprised, appearing to have forgotten that Harriet was there.

'Safety glass,' replied Abigail. 'We want to be able to protect the initials and explain to the visitors who they belong to.'

'So you're not removing the pew or replacing the shelf?'

'No!' Abigail sounded surprised. 'We're concerned that the constant touching by visitors will wear them away.'

Harriet nodded, trying hard to maintain a look of serious consideration.

'It's Harriet, isn't it?' James asked cautiously.

'Yes, why?'

'I believe you've volunteered here longer than anyone else. You must know quite a lot about the chapel, so do you know who HA was? We have our theories, but perhaps you've heard something.'

Harriet pretended to think for a moment.

'No, I've no idea, sorry.' She pulled herself up out of the pew and walked away down the aisle. She would miss running her fingers across the letters that Eric had created, each day she came to the chapel, but at least this way they would remain protected and on display for a very long time.

A FINAL VISIT

*R*oger Pickles took a deep breath before pulling himself up the stairs to the first floor of the cottage. His job as a security officer at Charleton House, the home of the Duke and Duchess of Ravensbury, meant he often walked several miles a day in the course of his duties, but it wasn't enough to counteract the effect of his wife's baking on his waistline. His steel-toe-capped boots clomped heavily on the bare wooden stairs as he ascended behind the elderly woman.

'Are you alright back there?' she asked, turning at the top of the stairs to check on him. 'I must have at least thirty years on you.' She grinned before disappearing into one of the rooms. Roger paused, took a deep breath, and made the final steps.

Roger had run into Sylvia Critchlow near the stables, where he'd dropped into the café for a cup of tea and a slice of chocolate cake. He was still licking chocolate off his fingers as she'd approached him, and he had realised who she was as soon as she had introduced herself. He'd heard her name before.

She'd grown up on the estate. Her father had been the stud groom for the 10th Duke of Ravensbury, the current Duke's grandfather, and her mother had worked in the kitchens as a cook. With her father's job had come a small cottage at the back of the stables. Now in her nineties, Sylvia had for many years returned to Charleton House and asked the security team if they'd be kind enough to allow her to take a look at her childhood home. On previous visits, she'd brought her children, then her grandchildren.

This was the first time that Roger had been on duty when she'd made an appearance, and he was keen to see the old place with her. The large bunch of keys hanging off his belt included a master key to the stable buildings, so he radioed his colleagues to tell them where he was going as he let Sylvia in. A low stone building, the cottage was kept neat and tidy outside, but the closed shutters on some of the windows and the moss growing on the roof and in the gutters made it clear it was no longer in use.

Roger peeked into a room to the left at the top of the stairs, a rather dated bathroom with fittings in avocado green. The floor tiles were chipped and the bath covered in bits of plaster that had fallen from the ceiling over time. He followed Sylvia into a room at the end of the landing and watched her from the doorway as she slowly ran the palm of her hand over the faded wallpaper. Patches of it were hanging off. The room was musty; not exactly damp, it was more as though Roger could smell the emptiness of the cottage.

'Daisies have always been my favourite flowers. When this became my bedroom, Father said that it would be decorated with whatever paper he could find. Years later, Mother told me that he had scoured every hardware store for miles around to find daisy wallpaper. He put it up when Mother took us to visit our grandparents for a weekend so it would be a surprise. I thought they were the brightest, prettiest daisies anywhere in the world. I tried to wake up early every day so that I could lie in bed and stare at them in the morning sun.'

'Were you born here?' Roger leant his bulk against the door frame.

'No, a couple of miles away. We moved in when Father got his promotion. I was eighteen months old.'

Roger looked around at the cobwebs. The windowsills were starting to rot; a pile of cables coiled on the floor in a corner. The Health and Safety department still considered the cottage to be safe, otherwise Security wouldn't be allowed to bring anyone in here, but how long that would last, Roger didn't know. He'd heard talk that the Duchess wanted to renovate it and rent it out to holidaymakers like she had other properties on the estate, but she'd need to get a move on before it fell down.

Sylvia was looking out of the window. Ahead, over a tall stone wall, lay the large kitchen garden. It was a warm day and visitors were strolling around the paths, looking at all manner of vegetables and fruit. Dahlias exploded in colour, with Sweet Williams and foxgloves keeping them company.

'My brother and I used to climb the wall and steal strawberries. We thought no one knew what we were up to, but of course the evidence was all over our clothes and round our mouths.' Sylvia looked back at Roger and stared at him intently. 'You look very familiar. I know we've not met here before, but I'm sure I've seen you somewhere else.'

Roger shrugged. 'I've a common enough face, you might have seen me in the shops.'

Sylvia shook her head. 'No, that's not it.' She moved towards the door and Roger stepped aside. She seemed even smaller when she got close to him, her slight frame engulfed by his shadow. Having not developed the stoop of some elderly people, she carried herself elegantly, but she appeared fragile, her delicate skin looking as though it would tear easily. Yet there was a look of concentration on her face and a certainty in her slate-blue eyes that told Roger she would bat away the hands of anyone who tried to help her unnecessarily.

He followed her back downstairs. She appeared satisfied with what she had seen in her old bedroom.

'Careful, love, watch that bottom step,' Roger called down as Sylvia led the way. 'I think it's getting a bit loose.'

'I'm quite alright,' she said firmly, her voice softening as she continued. 'If I had a bit more energy, I could run down these stairs without any bother.'

'I'll take your word for it, I don't need evidence.'

'Alright, Roger, for you, I'll repair at a dignified pace.'

Roger cursed himself for fussing. All the same, he could see her grip tighten on the bannister as she reached the last step. It didn't take much pressure for her knuckles to turn white. Roger lumbered down the stairs after her.

Like a bleedin' sack a' potatoes, he thought, opting not to risk the bottom step and landing with a thud on the lower floor.

The bare wooden floorboards were stained, but there were no signs of leaks in the ceiling so Roger assumed they were the marks left behind by previous occupants. Perhaps even a young Sylvia had spilt a jug of milk or glass of water. He couldn't see where she had gone, but then caught sight of her pale green skirt as she disappeared through a door, a swirl of dust caught in the sunlight behind her like a murmuration of starlings. Roger watched it settle before joining her.

She was standing in front of the kitchen sink. 'This was all modernised after we left. There was still an outside toilet when we moved in and Father would bathe in front of the fire in a big metal tub. I always wanted to help Mother fill it with water.' She grinned at him. 'I doubt you want to hear me ramble.'

'Lovin' it. I get to go to all sorts of places, there isn't a room I don't have a key to. When I'm on night patrol, I'll often stand in a room and wonder about the people who lived there: what they were like, what they said. I read stuff, of course, and I've had some chats with the Duke and Duchess, but only brief. When someone like you comes back, it's always nice to say hello, get a feel for the person, someone who lived here before it was like it is now.'

Sylvia looked a little confused.

'A business,' he confirmed. 'All the tourists, the gift shops, that kind of thing.'

'There must be some of us around, although I suppose we are dying out now. I've made it to my tenth decade.'

Roger whistled. 'If you don't mind me sayin', you don't look it.'

'Thank you, Roger, that's very kind.' She looked around the kitchen. 'It looks nothing like it did when I lived here, but the feel of the place still lingers. That's what matters; that's what I come back for.' She pointed at an old gas stove, the door of the oven hanging open. 'We had a big black beast of a thing, it dominated the room. I hated it, but it did keep the place nice and warm in the winter. Now, of course, I miss it, these modern things have no soul.'

Roger closed the door on the oven; he couldn't help himself. He turned around to see Sylvia staring at a pile of newspapers in the corner of the room.

'That's where it was! You were in the newspapers, last year.' She looked Roger firmly in the eyes. 'You won an award for saving that man. I'm in the presence of a hero.'

'I'm no such thing. I just helped out.'

'If I remember correctly, you did CPR on a dying man and saved his life. That makes you a hero in my book.'

Roger shrugged. 'I'm just glad I knew what to do.' He briefly pictured the car hurtling towards the gate at the edge of the Charleton estate as he checked on a colleague on duty there, it screeching to a halt, a woman flying out of the driving seat, screaming that her husband was having a heart attack. Roger and his colleague had jumped into action, pulling the man out of the car, Roger administering CPR while the other officer called for an ambulance. The man had survived, and the two security guards had been given a bravery award by the local police, but Roger wasn't a man to make a fuss about such things.

He changed the subject. 'Are you here on your own today?' he asked Sylvia.

'No, my family are on their way. I have about half an hour. Look at this old thing.' She pointed at a rotary dial phone on the wall, a layer of dust on the top. 'Something else from long after I left, but it's practically an antique now.'

She's right, thought Roger. He couldn't remember the last time he'd used a dial phone. These days it was all text messages; hardly anyone used a phone as an *actual* phone anymore.

'Have you seen this? A different kind of archeology.' Sylvia walked back into the hallway and pointed at a big patch on the wall where the wallpaper had been torn away to reveal more layers of paper behind. The room was papered in a grubby Anaglypta, dirt engrained around the lumps. The gash had revealed a pattern of delicate green leaves. In the midst of this, a smaller tear revealed a lavender-coloured paper.

'Paper through the ages,' she said. 'The sad thing is this top layer is the ugliest. I've always thought it looks like cottage cheese; glad it wasn't here during my time.' She looked at Roger. 'Oh dear, I hope you don't have this on your walls.'

Roger laughed. 'Not a chance, can't stand the stuff either.'

A silence followed, until Roger's curiosity got the better of him.

'Your dad was the stud groom, right? Did he have a lot to do with the Duke? What was he like?'

'He did indeed and was well respected by the Duke. In fact, he used to visit us here sometimes, the Duke. Mother would be furious if Father forgot to tell her he was coming, or didn't send someone ahead to warn her if it was a spur of the moment thing, and then she only had a few minutes to tidy the place up and prepare tea. The Duke was rather a stern-looking man. It took a long time for me to pluck up the courage to look him in the face;

I'd always look at his boots instead. I remember thinking he had enormous feet, not unlike yours.'

She smiled. 'I was afraid of him for many years, but he occasionally brought us gifts. My brother and I both received little wooden horses from him. He rarely smiled, but he loved his horses and he completely changed when he was around them. I often wondered if he wished he could give it all up in exchange for a simpler life.'

'Maybe he would have liked to have your father's job.'

'Oh yes, without a doubt.'

'Did you ever work at the house?'

'Not officially, but in 1939 I helped out when the mothers started to arrive.'

Roger knew immediately what she meant. After the start of the war, many of the rooms in Charleton House had been taken over by the Red Cross and used as a maternity hospital for expectant mothers evacuated from large cities like Sheffield and Manchester.

'I was only eleven when the war started, but I helped change the beds and prepare food. I'd talk to the mothers and give them some company. As I got older, I did more and more, even bathing some of the babies. I thought that was wonderful, but I felt so sorry for some of those girls, those ones who weren't married. They had it very tough.'

She seemed lost in thought, sad, but quickly shook herself out of it.

'There are many wonderful memories too, of course. The Duchess was often around, and my mother told me to pay close attention to how she spoke, that if I learnt to speak like her it would help me get on in the world. So, I took every opportunity to talk to her. I must have been quite irritating, but the Duchess never let it show. She even taught me a little French.'

They were back at the door and Roger let them out.

'When will we see you again?' he asked. Sylvia turned and

looked back into the cottage. This time the sadness was clear in her eyes, but her voice remained resolute.

'Oh, this is it, I'm afraid. It's time to say goodbye to the place.'

'That's a shame. If you change your mind, we'll be here to let you in.'

'Thank you, Roger, that's very kind, but it's time.'

She smiled before turning and walking back towards the stable block.

Two of Roger's colleagues were standing chatting outside the door to the security office when he arrived back.

'All good up at the cottage?' asked one, tattoos running the length of both of his arms.

'Aye.' Roger was distracted, still thinking of Sylvia. He'd liked her, a lot, and hoped that she would actually make it back. 'What you two up to?'

The shorter of the two men answered as he removed his peaked cap, giving the silver crest on it a quick polish before placing it firmly back on his head.

'Just waiting for the hearse, we've got that funeral this afternoon. The chaplain dropped one of these off, thought we'd like to see it seeing as a couple of us have met her. I'm going to attend on behalf of the security team.'

He passed Roger a folded card. On the front, below a photograph of a woman with slate-blue eyes, were the words:

A Service of Thanksgiving
for the life of
Sylvia Critchlow
21 May 1928– 18 August 2021
Charleton House Chapel
Tuesday 7 September 2021

A CHRISTMAS CONUNDRUM

*A*lice had just run past the door, followed closely by Tweedledum and Tweedledee. The Queen of Hearts strode confidently behind them.

A few minutes later the white rabbit sped by, shouting, 'Oh the irony... Hang on... I couldn't get my car to start... Wait...'

Still wearing a smart, long black coat, and a pair of velvet reindeer antlers on her head, Chelsea Morris dodged out of their way before sneaking into the Gilded Hall. At Christmas, it was her favourite room in Charleton House. The gilded balcony, after which the room was named, glowed warmly. The two Christmas trees that stood either side of a cavernous fireplace were decorated entirely with playing cards and hundreds of little white lights which glinted off Chelsea's long blonde hair. The room had been swathed in garlands made out of greenery from the grounds, and as part of the *Alice in Wonderland*-themed Christmas, little white rabbits and top hats hung from them. It had taken three weeks to get all the decorations up in the house and the end result was more than worth all the hard work.

Beside the magnificent staircase stood the tallest of the eighteen fir trees that could be found around the house. This was more traditionally decorated with red, gold and green baubles, although if you looked closely, you could see that many of them had been embellished with quotes from the text of *Alice in Wonderland*. Below the tree was a mountain of presents. It was a magical scene, the perfect vision of Christmas. Chelsea almost expected it to start snowing, despite her being indoors, or to hear the sound of Christmas carols.

Elsewhere in the building the Dodo had taken up residence in the library, and the dining room had been set for the Mad Hatter's party. Life-size characters were seated ready for tea, while the Hatter himself posed in the middle of the table, raising his hat into the air, a magnificent expression of jubilation on his face. From behind a locked door came the sound of the ill-tempered cook throwing objects around the kitchen and refusing to give evidence at the trial.

The Great Chamber now had a giant chess set at its centre. There were *Alice in Wonderland* costumes for both adults and children alike to wear to take photographs. Chelsea had tried a few on, the resultant photos becoming the Christmas cards that she had sent to family and friends.

Chelsea was an assistant in the Library Café who had been given the chance to take on more responsibility by her manager, Sophie Lockwood. She was only twenty, but had a maturity beyond her years. At first she had eagerly grabbed the opportunity, but now she was less sure. Tonight was a relatively small Christmas event for an audience of 100 children and their families, all of whom had won a range of competitions in order to be here. The event started off outdoors, and in a short while a big spotlight would shine upon the roof and Father Christmas would appear over the parapet before seeming to disappear down a chimney. After that, the guests would be welcomed into the house by the Duke and Duchess before Father Christmas joined them to distribute presents. It required a bit of energy on his part, but it had run smoothly in previous years. In the meantime, the children and their families were enjoying a light show which illuminated the front of the house with festive images to the backdrop of Christmas music. Alice and her friends wandered about, entertaining them and encouraging them to play croquet with giant plastic flamingos. It was a crisp winter evening and everyone was bundled up, hot drinks and the buzz of excitement keeping them warm.

There wasn't a great deal for Chelsea to look after: a few outdoor food stands serving hot chocolate and mulled wine, while gourmet burgers, sausages and a hog roast were available for those who were particularly hungry. The aroma of roasting chestnuts filled the air. Most of these stalls could take care of themselves, but Chelsea was there to offer support and deal with any complaints from customers. Sophie had promised that she would keep her mobile phone with her in case Chelsea had any questions, but she was determined to show that she could cope, and so far it had been going smoothly. The worst she'd had to deal with was someone who decided that an apple and chestnut pork sausage was too porky and she had simply refunded them, wondering how Sophie dealt with this sort of thing on a daily basis.

She must have the patience of a saint, Chelsea concluded.

With everything under control, she'd returned to the house and had quickly ducked into the Gilded Hall to take another look at the decorations. Mark Boxer, the most experienced and senior of the house tour guides, was already in the room when Chelsea had crept in and was standing in front of the fireplace. She hadn't spotted him straight away and jumped as he started to speak.

'I believe that the 10th Duke got stuck trying to climb up here one Christmas.' He leaned a hand on the chimney breast. 'He was drunk, of course, and decided it would be fun to come tumbling out when his mother had guests in here for drinks. When I was a student, I got drunk, stole a traffic cone and stuck it on Prince Albert's head. A little more pedestrian.'

'Sorry?' Chelsea had always found Mark rather intimidating. He seemed to know something about everything and he had an air of peering down his nose at people. Chelsea was convinced he didn't like her very much.

'The statue of Prince Albert in Albert Square, Manchester. I stuck a traffic cone on his head.'

She didn't know what to say to that and decided that keeping quiet was the best way to go. Leaving Mark to his thoughts, she walked over to the Christmas tree at the bottom of the stairs. She had watched a team of staff manoeuvre the 25-foot-tall tree into position and was very pleased that she hadn't been involved; she would probably have knocked over a statue or broken a window. Chelsea was tall and could be clumsy, still trying to work out what to do with her long limbs.

She took a deep breath through her nose, trying to take in as much of the fir tree aroma as possible. The mountain of fake presents under its branches were all beautifully wrapped with glittery ribbon and enormous bows, but there was one gift that hadn't been wrapped. Chelsea felt rather sorry for whoever it was intended for, and then reminded herself that none of them were real. These looked real, though: black boots.

She took a closer look. The boots had warm-looking white fluffy trims around the top, and beyond them a pair of rather chunky red legs. She let out a yelp and clambered round the side of the tree, squeezing herself along beside the staircase to get a better view.

'Oh my... it's... HELP! It's Father Christmas, he's...' She crawled further into the tree, crushing the presents. 'I think he's dead.'

Mark's face peered at her from amongst the branches.

'What are you squawking about? Father Christmas is... Oh my God, is he dead?'

'I think so.' Chelsea felt his neck for a pulse before realising that she had never done a first aid course and had only a rough idea where it might be. He looked as if he was fast asleep and smelt of what Chelsea called 'old man mints'. Peering at him more closely, she saw that he was bleeding from the top of his head. It was hard to tell amongst all the white hair, but it looked as though he had quite a long, deep cut.

Someone had given Father Christmas an almighty bash on the head.

'He's still alive.' Roger Pickles, a security guard, was leaning over the body of Father Christmas. 'Someone pass me that first aid kit, I'll try and keep the wound clean and stop the bleeding until the ambulance gets here. I think he might have broken his arm as well, it's at a very strange angle. Did anyone see what happened?'

Chelsea shook her head, even though Roger couldn't see her from his position amongst the branches of the tree.

'No,' Mark answered for her. 'Do you know who he is?'

'Father Christmas, I reckon,' replied Roger without a hint of amusement. Mark tipped his head back and looked about to make a biting comment, but Chelsea got there first.

'Is he *the* Father Christmas?'

'The one and only,' replied Mark with a roll of the eyes.

'I mean,' said Chelsea, equally acerbically, any intimidation she may have felt in Mark's presence forgotten, 'the Father Christmas for tonight.'

'Aye.' Roger was tucked so far into the branches, it gave the impression the Christmas tree was talking. 'It's Frank Broom. He used to work with us in security before he retired; he's come back each year since to do this. Oh bleedin' 'ell, the Duchess'll be wondering where he's got to. Someone needs to find a replacement and sharpish. I'll leave that to you two.'

For a moment, Chelsea froze. She was meant to be looking after the food stalls, but then no one had tried to contact her on the radio she was carrying so that presumably meant everything was okay. She told herself to think. This was not the hardest thing she had ever dealt with. She needed a man, and not just because she didn't have a date for New Year's Eve. Finding one turned out to be very easy.

Chelsea turned to face Mark.

'What? Oh no, I'm not climbing on the roof, then being mauled by a gang of screaming kids. Forget it.'

'You've no choice. The Duchess needs a Father Christmas and she needs one *now*.'

'No way. It's thanks to that woman that I once appeared on national television dressed up as a historically inaccurate William Shakespeare with a codpiece that could have doubled as a shopping bag. I'm not doing that again.'

'There are no cameras, no codpieces and you won't be attacked. Plus the Duchess will be forever grateful, I'm sure.'

'Well, we don't have a costume, unless you plan on stripping an unconscious body.'

'Yes, we do. Chef Gregg dresses up as Santa for his nephews' school and they had their party yesterday. It's hanging in Sophie's office.'

Mark closed his eyes and dropped his head, muttering, 'I hope you've got an especially large cushion. I'm not sure the kids will believe you if you tell them Father Christmas has been on a diet since last year.'

Chelsea looked at his skinny frame. 'I'll fetch two.'

'What in the name of all that is holy…?'

Chelsea looked up from her job of stuffing newspaper into Mark's trousers. Over at the Christmas tree, Father Christmas was being lifted onto a stretcher by two paramedics, and just inside the door – and asking the question – was Bill Asquith, Mark's husband. Behind him stood Detective Constable Joe Greene, who also happened to be Bill's brother, and a police officer in uniform who, after a quiet word from Joe, remained at the door.

'What are you doing here?' Mark asked. 'I was really hoping that no one I know would see me being packed into this ridiculous outfit.'

'Packed is the operative word,' said Bill, sniggering. 'Need a hand, Chelsea? I reckon you're going to need a full month's worth of newspapers to make him look like anything other than an extremely emaciated cousin of our good Saint Nick.'

'Oh, be quiet and pass me the beard and hat,' grumbled Mark. 'Why are you here anyway?'

'I'm here to give you a lift home, remember? You reversed your car into the plastic reindeers outside the garden centre and Rudolph cracked the back windscreen.'

'I was trying to forget that.'

'I wish I'd seen it,' said Joe. 'I'd love to have arrested you for dangerous driving.'

'Haven't you got cat burglars to chase across rooftops?' Mark asked his brother-in-law.

'Seriously? You've got an unconscious Father Christmas over there, which happens to be the reason that a poor innocent young woman is shoving her hands down your trousers, and you're asking about cat burglars? I'm here because the information I've received says he's been given a heck of a clout on the head. So, if you'll excuse me, I have a job to do. Chelsea, I suggest you seek psychological counselling when you've finished that.'

'What are you smirking at?' Mark asked her.

'I've got my hands down your trousers, you should be nicer to me.' Chelsea paused; she wasn't sure where the confidence had come from to say that. 'I mean, I'm...' but Mark laughed out loud, and kept laughing.

'I can't believe this is happening,' he said as he took a breath. 'And you need to say that sort of thing more often. Well, not that exact thing because I hope this won't happen again, but I like snarky Chelsea.' He turned to look at Bill. 'And you can stop laughing. You should try… Hang on, my sweet, darling husband, who is extraordinarily handsome and has the most perfect slightly rounded – well, largely rounded – belly, possibly the nicest belly this side of the North Pole…'

Bill, a retired professional rugby player who Chelsea noted was actually pretty fit looking, apart from a slightly rotund stomach that paid testament to a love of food, stopped laughing and glared at his husband.

'Not a chance. I don't even work here.'

'Nor did Frank. He was retired and helping out. Come on – you're a teacher. You love kids, and you know how to deal with them. You'll have no problem on the roof, and let's be honest, I'll make a pretty useless Father C.'

'You'll make a bleeding awful one.' Bill looked imploringly at Chelsea, but Mark was right. She agreed Bill would be perfect for the job.

'Give it all to me.'

Mark pulled his trousers off, scattering newspaper every-where, and landed a big kiss on Bill's cheek.

'I love you, I love you, I love you!'

'You owe me, you owe me, you owe me,' was Bill's response.

'Chelsea?'

The young woman left the couple getting Bill into his outfit and joined Joe, who had just finished talking to the paramedics.

'You found him here, under the tree?'

'Yes. I only came in to look at the decorations and I saw his boots.'

'You didn't see or hear anyone else? You didn't pass anyone leaving the room?'

'No, no one. It was just Mark and me in here.'

'Okay, well it looks like he fell off these stairs. At least, that's how I think he broke his arm. That cut on the head, though, that looks like someone attacked him. The paramedics agree, and also think it happened very recently, within the last hour. Mark!'

Mark stopped helping Bill into his Father Christmas boots and came over. 'You summoned me?'

'Chelsea says you were already in here when she arrived. Did you see anyone else? Did anyone leave while you were here?'

'So you don't think this was an accident?'

'Unlikely.'

'No one. I was in here for about half an hour before Chelsea arrived. Before that, the room was locked,' he dangled a set of keys in the air, 'and I was outside the door, talking to the Duke. He was on his way to join the Duchess, but I think he was delaying. He's as keen on a roomful of children as I am.'

'How long were you outside the door?'

'About forty minutes, which I presume means the attacker didn't enter or exit this way?'

'Agreed. Thanks.'

'My pleasure. Now if you don't mind, I need to lead the big man up onto the roof.'

Joe turned back to Chelsea. 'Are the kids being brought in here?'

'No, they won't come anywhere near here. They're taking them into the New Gallery, just off the shop. There's not as much in there that can be damaged and they've gone to town on the decorations.'

'Okay, that should be fine. I'll tell security to make sure no one comes any further in than that, which should keep my detective sergeant happy.'

Joe turned to look at Roger, who had just walked down the stairs, his forehead heavily creased.

'Alright, Roger? You look like you need a sit down.'

'Think I've found where it happened, or what they were after, or... well, sort of...'

'You're not making much sense. Show me, and don't touch anything.'

Roger led the way and Joe followed. Chelsea wasn't sure if she was meant to join them, but curiosity got the better of her, and Joe didn't attempt to stop her as she climbed the stairs behind the two men.

Roger led them into a long corridor of rooms with a railway carriage layout. The doors separating each room were in line with each other at one side of the building, so it was possible to stand with them all open and see all the way through to the far end, five rooms away. As they walked along, Chelsea gradually saw more and more evidence of a disturbance. In one room, a chair had been knocked over; in the next, books had fallen off a table. Each room was in a slightly worse state than the last and the furthest room was a scene of chaos.

A series of ropes attached to brass posts, which were meant to keep the public away from the furniture and valuable objects, were now lying snake-like on the floor. Beyond them was a scene that made Chelsea go cold. A large painting had come off the wall and was now leaning awkwardly against a chair which had ripped through the canvas. She bent down and saw that the painting was a portrait of an unattractive man with a long curly wig and burgundy-red coat. Feeling as though he was peering back at her, she quickly stood up and stepped back.

Silverware was scattered around. Chelsea nearly tripped over a large silver jug, a dent clearly visible in it. The rug was rucked up into a pile in the middle of the space. It looked like the scene of a bar brawl.

Roger whistled. 'This breaks my heart, it does. The Duke and Duchess will be gutted when they're told.'

'Ugh, something I'll leave to the boss,' said Joe. Roger didn't look impressed with him wimping out, but Chelsea wouldn't have wanted that job either.

'Has anything been taken?' asked Joe, pulling out a notebook. Roger scanned the room.

'Not that I can immediately see, but we'd have to check the inventory. I'll radio the security office and tell them they're going to need to call out someone who knows this room better than us. And you might need to put your big-boy pants on and tell the Duke and Duchess.'

Chelsea sniggered. She couldn't have said it better herself.

'Okay,' Joe either hadn't heard or was ignoring the dig, 'we need to seal off this area, and then we can wait for DS Harnby to arrive. Chelsea, do you reckon you can make us some coffee and tea back in the café? I'll make sure security are clear on the areas they need to cordon off until I get more officers over here.'

'Wait.' Chelsea strode over to a windowsill. On its side, almost rolling off onto the floor, was an empty vodka bottle. She knew better than to pick it up. Roger gave a big sigh and looked at Joe.

'Do you think this was kids? Older ones who tagged along with their families and snuck off to have a drink in the grounds of the house, then thought it would be fun to try and get in? If they were drunk and Frank disturbed 'em, they might have panicked and attacked him.'

'How would they have got in?'

'Not sure, but this ain't the Tower of London. It wouldn't be the first time someone has been able to hide themselves away when we were locking up, or climbed over a wall and found themselves stumbling into areas that are meant to be secure. Not that I should say that, of course, we do our best to make sure this place is secure. It's just that... well, you know how it is.'

Chelsea wasn't surprised by any of this. She'd heard the stories about visitors who had been found wandering around after hours and had no idea they'd been locked in.

'Great.' There was a large dollop of sarcasm in Joe's voice. 'If it was kids, then chances are they've scarpered and we'll be hard pressed to find them. Let's just hope they've left fingerprints on that bottle.'

'There is one other thing.'

Chelsea looked at Roger. She wanted a cup of tea – couldn't his question wait until they got to the cafe?

'Frank's son, Lee, is a bit of a troublemaker. He's got a record, and I know he likes a drink.'

'What kind of record?' asked Chelsea, her curiosity immediately piqued as her yearning for tea was forgotten. She then glanced up at Joe with an apologetic look.

'It's a good question,' he conceded.

'GBH and burglary, amongst other things. He was a busy lad. He got a prison sentence.'

Joe was rapidly taking notes as Roger spoke. 'Is he still inside?'

'No, he's been out at least a year. Frank said he'd turned over a new leaf, wanted to be a better dad to his kids. Also…'

'What? Come on, Rog,' Chelsea encouraged him.

'Frank asked if we could get him a couple of tickets for tonight. Not for the indoor part, but the lightshow and stuff outside. Said Lee wanted to bring his kids.'

'So he's here on site?' Joe asked, with what looked to Chelsea like a gleam in his eye.

'I reckon so.'

'Great! It'll make the boss's day if we can find him and get this sorted quickly.'

'But why would he want to attack his own dad?' asked Chelsea.

Joe shrugged. 'He has a track record of violence and theft. Maybe they don't have a great relationship, or his dad got between Lee and something valuable. It wouldn't be the first time the victim is related to the attacker.'

The thought of a son doing that to his dad brought Chelsea back down to earth with a bump. It would be so tragic.

Roger gave her arm a quick squeeze. 'Come on, love, let's get a hot drink.'

Chelsea led the way down a dark wooden staircase that led off the most vandalised of the rooms. Both Roger and Joe were on their phones and radios, making calls to try to track down Lee amongst the crowd outside. Even if he wasn't responsible, he needed to know that his father had been injured and was on his way to hospital.

Chelsea heard a burst of shouts and claps. She guessed that Bill had just appeared on the roof of the building, following the sound of reindeer bells and hoofs, and the kids were all very excited at having finally seen Father Christmas. She was more than a little disappointed that Mark had got out of that; she'd have loved to have got a photo of him clambering over the roof to show her boss Sophie, who happened to be Mark's best friend. He'd have looked like a coat hanger wrapped in red velvet.

As they neared the bottom of the stairs, Chelsea felt a blast of cold air. It was always freezing down here, descending into a stone corridor, and the doors at either end were old and draughty, leading out to gardens on one side and a courtyard on the other. On a night like this, it formed an icy cold wind tunnel, and as they reached the bottom of the stairs, she could see that both doors were wedged open. That didn't help. Electrical cables in big thick rubber tubes trailed along the corridor and out into the gardens. They had been pushed back along the edge of the far wall to stop anyone tripping over them.

Joe stopped and looked at Roger. 'Is the corridor always left open like this?'

'For events, if we need it for things like lighting.' He nodded at the cables. 'This is all for the light show and to make sure Father Christmas can be seen clearly.'

'Is no one guarding these doors? Surely anyone could come and go from the garden. All you'd need to do is hop over the wall, come through here, and then go up the stairs. Don't tell me those stairs are unlocked all the time?'

'Not all the time, no, but we knew that Frank was using them as a shortcut. He knows the place better than me; he worked here for forty years, so he could time his routes down to the second. He has a set of keys and we would turn the alarms off when we knew he was going up.'

'And these doors?' Joe indicated towards the garden.

'They get locked too, but if we can't, like tonight, then we have a security officer here making sure no one comes in or out without permission.'

'So where are they?'

'You looking for me?' A stocky security officer, so heavily bundled up in a scarf and hat that Chelsea could only see his eyes, appeared out of the gloom. 'Alright, Rog, got a problem?'

Joe explained what had happened while Chelsea felt the cold crawl deeper inside her.

'Bloody Nora!' the guard exclaimed once Joe had finished. 'I saw Frank head up. I was round the corner, watching him; it looked like he was struggling to get the right key in the lock, so I was gonna help, but he got it open before I reached him and went inside.'

'Did you see anyone after that?' Joe asked.

'Not a dicky bird. I've been down here ever since and not seen no one till you lot came down.'

'Didn't you hear anything? A lot of damage was done up there.'

The guard shook his head.

'Nothin'. But you've got two heavy wooden doors between me and up there, plus it's a couple of floors up. Oh, and...' Grinning, he pulled off his woolly hat to reveal a pair of pink ear muffs. 'My girl wanted to make sure her dad was warm.' He pointed at a small earpiece 'This means I don't miss any radio calls, but I'll be honest, I can't hear much else unless you're right in front of me, like now.'

'Okay, can you make sure no one else goes in? I'll get a uniform over here.'

'Aye, aye.' The security guard touched his forehead with a finger in a salute as the small group crossed the courtyard.

'He's a good man, is Mike. If he says he didn't see anyone, then he definitely didn't see anyone.' Roger sounded confident about his colleague. 'But how the heck did whoever did this get in, or out?'

Joe stopped. 'What other doors are there into that area?'

'There's one behind the staircase in the Gilded Hall, but that's sealed up. We had a leak on the other side yesterday and everything's being protected or cleaned. It would be dead easy to tell if the plywood or plastic sheets have been disturbed.'

As Roger spoke, Chelsea felt herself shiver, but it had nothing to do with the cold.

'Is the attacker still in there? Were they in there when we walked through?'

Joe put a hand on her shoulder. 'Chelsea, you head back to the café. Roger and I need to go and have another look.'

When Detective Sergeant Colette Harnby walked into the café, she was wearing a red sweater with Rudolph the Reindeer staring out from it. His nose was twinkling with a red light that had been stitched into the wool.

'Don't say a word,' she ordered everyone in the room. 'I meant to leave it in the car. I'll get changed in a minute. So, I believe someone attacked Santa. Joe, can you tell me what's been going on? Then you can show me where it happened.'

Chelsea left them to it and busied herself making some drinks. This wasn't quite what she had signed up for when she agreed to take on more responsibility. She knew that Sophie had a habit of stumbling across dead bodies, but Chelsea had never considered that it might be part of the job description.

After a while, Chelsea realised that she knew Frank. Not to talk to, but he'd drop by and have a coffee in the security office with whoever was on duty. He seemed nice enough; it was so unfair this would happen to a harmless old man who was trying to make Christmas extra special for a group of children.

She was thinking about the bottle of vodka as she took a plate of ginger biscuits out to Joe and Harnby.

'Are you sure you've checked everywhere?' the sergeant was asking.

'Everywhere. In cupboards, under tables, there's no sign of anyone.' Joe looked exhausted, but smiled warmly at Chelsea as she placed the plate on the table. 'The door behind the staircase is secure too. Roger and I went over it with a fine-tooth comb, but none of the sealant has been torn, no tape has been pulled off. The plywood is undisturbed. I don't see how anyone could have used that as a way in or out, and then left it looking so untouched.'

'What about the windows?' Chelsea asked.

Joe shook his head. 'All secure, from the inside.'

Harnby sat back in her chair. She'd retrieved a small fake tea light from the table decoration and was switching it on and off as she stared ahead.

'So we've got a Santa who's been attacked in a part of the house that was locked and we've no idea how someone got in or out. Are there any magicians performing at tonight's kids' party?'

'I wish there were, it might explain things,' replied Joe.

'Okay, well let's think about the "who" for a while. It might help us figure out the "how" if we can identify who did this.'

Joe's phone rang and he nodded as he listened to the caller.

'They've found Lee, Frank's son. He's upset that we're accusing him of attacking his father, but he seems more bothered that we're ruining his night out and says he was with his kids the whole time.'

Harnby stood up. 'I want to talk to him. Tell them I'll head to the security office.'

Chelsea wondered if she'd remember to change her sweater before interviewing a suspect. If not, would Rudolph be good cop or bad cop?

Chelsea spent the next hour outside, helping the stallholders pack up and making sure nothing was left behind. By the time she made it back into the café, her fingertips had gone numb and she couldn't wait to wrap her hands around a hot mug. Harnby arrived back in the Library Café at the same time as Chelsea, no longer wearing the reindeer sweater, having swapped it for a plain black polo neck. She was looking less than pleased.

'Not only is Lee on the security cameras, enjoying a bag of roasted chestnuts around the time his father was attacked, but he's been sober since he went into prison. He insisted on being breathalysed, so I got one of the uniform lads to do it. Couldn't be used as evidence, but it came up negative. The vodka bottle isn't his.'

'I guess that would have been too neat,' replied Joe.'

'Kids?' asked Harnby.

'We thought about that. It's not impossible, but if they'd been mucking around in the courtyards, then they'd have been spotted by security. And we still don't know how they got in. How did the Duke and Duchess take it?'

'Yeah, thanks for that, Joe. You could have gone and spoken to them yourself rather than waiting until I arrived. I know I'm the senior officer, but you've met them often enough. Usual response: very concerned and keen to do all they can to help. I told them the best thing they could do is make sure the event goes off smoothly, and then get everyone off site and home. They have the contact details of everyone who has tickets, so if we need to track them down, we can.'

'What about the painting, or any of the other objects?'

Harnby and Joe turned to look at Chelsea, who hadn't been able to stop herself from chipping in.

'What do you mean? It didn't look like anything had been stolen.' Joe looked confused.

'Well, maybe something in that room is on some sort of wanted list. Like, lots of art by the same artist is being stolen right now... what do you call it? Stolen to order? Only Frank disturbed the burglar before they could take it.'

Harnby's face lit up. 'That's not a bad idea. There's a DC over in Buxton who has a real interest in that sort of thing. We can ask him.'

Chelsea felt buoyed by Harnby's response; she'd been worried it was a stupid thing to say. As she stepped away from the table, she almost backed into Roger.

'Cup of tea, Rog?'

'Please, Chelsea. I was wondering if anyone has heard how Frank is doing?' Roger looked over towards Joe and Harnby. Joe shook his head.

'Sorry, Roger, I haven't, but I'll find out and let you know.'

'I appreciate it. It's awful what happened. He was in such a good mood when he arrived. Having been at the pub, he was running late; he jumped out of the taxi, gave me a big wave, shouted, "Happy Christmas, mate," and dashed through the gate with his Santa suit over his arm.'

Chelsea poured a mug of tea from the large pot on the table and handed it to Roger along with a couple of gingerbread snowmen. 'These will help you through the night shift.'

'Thanks, love, very good of you.' They walked back together towards the counter, leaving Joe looking thoughtful.

'Can I have a quick word, Roger?'

He looked at Chelsea with concern. 'Of course, what's up?'

She pulled him to one side, out of earshot of the detectives. 'Did Frank seem okay to you? You said he'd been to the pub – was he drunk?'

'Why, do you think it matters?'

'I'm trying to understand why he didn't call for help when he came across whoever attacked him. He had a mobile and one of your radios, so why didn't he call? You've said he was a great security officer, but if he was drunk, maybe he thought he could take them on. If he wasn't drunk, then that might mean something else, like he knew them and was trying to reason with them.'

'You mean his son?'

'Well unless Lee has a twin, I guess not, but he knew a lot of people from here, right? Other staff. Did he get on with everyone when he worked here?'

'Absolutely. Everyone liked him. I can't imagine anyone wanting to hurt him.'

'And was he?'

'What?'

'Drunk?'

'No, not that I could tell.'

'What are you not telling me, Roger?'

'Well, I never spoke to him.' Roger was avoiding Chelsea's eye. 'He shouted hello, but we didn't have a conversation. I'd already told him we'd leave his radio and keys on the counter in reception, which is unattended at that time of night, so he grabbed those and ran off to get changed. He looked okay.'

'So he *could* have been drunk?'

'I 'spose so. Does it really make a difference?'

'Oh, I don't know. I'm just thinking out loud.'

Chelsea was ready to sit down and take a break, but the next person to walk through the door put paid to that idea.

'What are the chances you have something strong and entirely unsuitable for children?'

Distracted by the flat cap he was now wearing, Chelsea took a minute to realise what Mark was talking about. He looked as if he should be delivering newspapers and wearing short trousers. She also couldn't help noticing that his moustache had little wisps of white fluff stuck to it, remnants of the Father Christmas outfit before Bill had relieved him of his festive duties.

'There might be an open half bottle of wine, but I don't know if it will be any good.'

'I really don't care if it tastes like petrol, I need something to deaden the memory of a hundred screaming little people, all jacked up on sugar, running towards me. I made the near fatal error of standing in the doorway while they all watched my sexy Santa wave from the roof. Once he vanished, I was suddenly the only object between them and the New Gallery where his grotto had been set up. I'm surprised I didn't end up in the same condition as Frank. How is he, anyway? Able to name his attacker yet?'

Joe shook his head. 'We have an officer at the hospital and they'll let us know when he regains consciousness.'

After hunting in the storeroom, Chelsea found the half-empty bottle of white wine in the fridge. She had no idea how long it had been there. Mark looked longingly at the large glass that Chelsea placed in front of him.

'Ta, much appreciated. Was much damage done?'

Joe listed some of the displaced objects that had been immediately identified.

'Old Admiral Tom, eh? Well, it seems rather appropriate.'

Chelsea's confusion must have been written on her face as, after Mark had glanced up at her, he explained.

'Lord Admiral Thomas Fitzwilliam-Scott. He was the 2nd Duke's youngest brother and a bit of a black sheep in some ways. He rose rapidly through the ranks of the Royal Navy, but as far as I can tell, he drank his way around the world. At Charleton

House, he's most famous for a Christmas bash he threw in 1701. The Duke and his family were away for Christmas and the Admiral decided to hold a four-day party.

'On Christmas Day, he had one of the courtyard fountains filled with 1,000 litres of punch. Cups of the stuff were served by a little boy who floated around the fountain on a boat. Things eventually got messy when a group of guests – led by the Admiral – pulled off their shoes and stockings and climbed into the fountain, almost drowning the little boy. After that, they went on a rampage – a couple of them completely starkers – around the house, damaging a number of precious objects and a couple of paintings, including one of the Admiral's father, who he'd never got on particularly well with. So it does seem that what happened tonight is a particularly appropriate display of karma.

'Quite why someone would want to steal that painting, though, I have no idea. It's not a great piece of work and he's not a good-looking chap. Always seems a bit suspicious to me, kind of picture where you feel the eyes are following you around the room. I wouldn't trust him as far as I could throw him, man or portrait.'

Chelsea liked the concept of a fountain that dispensed alcohol, but in a more demure way than the one the Admiral had put together. One with taps, where good-quality wine was poured into a glass without a child nearly drowning. She had experienced the occasional unruly guest at a wedding or a conference, but things were much more civilised at Charleton House these days: no drunken rampages, no one running around in their birthday suit. At least, no one over the age of two.

'What's next?' Mark asked Joe.

'Now I know Frank was at the pub before he came here, I'm going to head over there and see if anyone noticed something. Maybe he annoyed someone and they followed him; maybe the attacker worked here and could come in without raising suspicion; maybe they arrived ahead of him and waited for him, although that still doesn't explain how they got out.'

Chelsea thought about Frank getting drunk in a Santa suit. Only a little while later, he was due to clamber along a roof and entertain children who were the guests of a very notable aristocratic family. Some people really did have poor judgement.

'Right, well I reckon I'll go and see how Bill is getting on. I can't go home without him now we've only got one car, and I can judge how strong a drink I'll need to pour him when we get back.' Mark reached for the bag that he'd tucked under the table, banging his head on the corner as he sat back up and knocking the flat cap off. 'Owwwww!' he cried out dramatically. 'Who put that damn thing there?'

Joe sniggered, and then made an exaggerated show of biting his lip.

'Haven't you a crime to go and solve, rather than knocking the afflicted?' Mark growled as he picked up the flat cap.

'Why are you wearing that thing anyway?' asked Joe, still smirking. 'You look like an extra from *Oliver*.'

'Because putting on Santa's wig ruined my hair and I can't find my emergency pomade; I must have left it in my car. This will cover up a multitude of sins until I can get home.'

Mark was right. His usually perfect hair was rather flat and held some of the same wisps of white fluff as his moustache.

Mark donned his cap, and then looked at Chelsea. 'What are you staring at? Does it not look right?' He pulled it to the left. 'Better? No, how about this?' He pulled it a little to the right. 'Say something, girl. Have I made it better or worse?'

Chelsea dragged herself from her thoughts. Something was tugging at her brain, but Mark seemed determined to distract her.

'I think you should try pulling it forward, all the way forward.' Mark adjusted it. 'No, further, all the way. Keep going, further down...'

'Ha, ha, very funny,' Mark replied sarcastically from under the low brim. 'Chelsea, just tell me if it looks okay.'

Instead of answering, she turned to Joe. 'I don't think you need to bother going to the pub.'

'Why not?'

'Are we allowed back upstairs? I think I know what happened.'

Joe looked over at DS Harnby.

'Forensics have finished in the end room, so I don't see why not.'

Chelsea and the two detectives made their way across the courtyard, down the cold stone corridor and back up the wooden stairs.

'What are you thinking?' Harnby asked a rather nervous Chelsea once they'd climbed the stairs and were standing in the doorway. Now they were there, she wasn't so sure. Perhaps her idea was ridiculous.

'It was the story that Mark told about the Admiral in the picture. The drunken party. Look at the room. It looks like a fight happened, someone was pushed around, furniture was knocked over. Only I don't think there was a fight and no one was pushed around. It sounds crazy, but I think the Admiral did it. The Admiral attacked Frank.'

Joe and Harnby looked at her as though she had just dropped in from another planet.

'What on earth...?'

'Hear me out. If Frank was drunk, then he could have stumbled as he came up the stairs and into the room. As he stepped into the ropes, the posts came crashing down and he tripped, knocking into the painting. That fell off the wall and hit him on the head. He was concussed, and as he staggered along, he ended up bumping into all sorts of things. That's why there are things on the floor in most of these rooms: he couldn't steady himself.

As he reached the top of the stairs, in a drunken and dizzy state, he tumbled over the edge and onto the Christmas presents.'

Joe looked fascinated. Harnby looked at Chelsea as if she was a madwoman, and she regretted saying anything. But, she could picture the whole thing: Frank finishing off the vodka, unable to steady himself.

Chelsea looked at the painting, which had been leant up against the wall. The hole had removed half his face so the Admiral now looked at them with a slightly odd expression. There were signs of his arrogance in the half of the face that was still visible, the corner of his lip slightly curled up. It appeared to Chelsea that he was sniggering at them.

'I reckon that you'll find Frank's blood on that frame, and little bits of wood and maybe even gilding in his wound.'

'So we're not looking for anyone else? Father Christmas just had a few too many?' Joe looked a bit nonplussed as he answered his ringing phone. 'Excuse me.' He walked into the next room to take the call.

'You've got an officer at the hospital, right?' Chelsea asked and Harnby nodded. 'Could you ask him to talk to the doctors, see if they found anything when they were cleaning him up?' Harnby, a disbelieving look on her face, pulled out her phone all the same.

By the time Joe had hung up and walked back over to them, Harnby had also finished her call. They glanced at one another.

'Okay,' said Harnby, 'there were a couple of tiny pieces of wood found in Frank's wound.' She took a breath. 'And one of them had gold on one side.'

Chelsea felt her shoulders relax. Her stomach was still in a knot, but it was a start.

It was Joe's turn. 'That was the officer at the pub. One of Frank's mates had just become a grandfather for the first time, so the drinks were flowing. Frank had a couple and was pretty merry when he left, after the winners of a raffle that was being held for a local charity had been announced.'

'Don't tell me,' said Harnby, 'he won a bottle of vodka.'

Chelsea looked at the now one-eyed Admiral. He'd almost killed a man from beyond the grave.

'I'm sorry, Chelsea, I thought it was going to be a relatively straightforward night.' Sophie had invited Chelsea to join her for coffee the next morning.

'Don't apologise, you didn't know what would happen.'

'True, but still, it was a bit much for your first night being in charge. Next time, I'll make sure it's quieter.'

She smiled and Chelsea laughed.

'Wouldn't it be nice if you had that power… wait, next time? So, you'll let me do it again?'

'All sorts of things could have gone wrong with the catering, but nothing as bad as finding an unconscious, injured and, it turns out, drunk Father Christmas. You kept your cool, made sure there was a stand-in Father Christmas and figured out what had happened before the police did. You should be running the whole shebang; I reckon I could take a week off and leave you in charge.'

'Please don't,' begged Chelsea. The more she thought about it, the more she liked the idea of having some responsibility, but she could do without the additional drama.

'Okay, well not the whole shebang, but how about a bit more responsibility?'

'Is there another small event coming up?'

'No, but I never filled that assistant supervisor's role that came up at the end of the summer. I didn't think I needed to worry about it until next Easter when the numbers of visitors will rise sharply, but I am starting to feel the pinch. You'd report in to Tina as the Library Café supervisor and be her right-hand woman. She'll be a great teacher and I really do think you'd be perfect.'

Chelsea wasn't sure what to say.

'You taking it, then?' Mark lowered his wiry frame into a chair and Sophie raised her eyes to the ceiling.

'Mark, you have the subtlety of a sledgehammer. I've only just asked her.'

'Well, I think you should take it. If you can deal with a dead Santa, then you can deal with whatever the customers here throw at you.'

'He wasn't dead,' Chelsea pointed out.

'No, but we thought he was in the beginning, and you didn't start flapping. You just got on with things. In fact, you were rather confident; might I say a tad on the cocky side?' He looked at her out of the corner of his eye and gave his moustache a twist.

'I'm so sorry, Mark, I didn't mean to overstep the mark. I mean… I didn't…'

'Don't ruin it. I love that side of you. Just don't aim it at me too often. So, that's agreed, then. She's taking the job.'

'Are you?' Sophie gave her a hopeful look. Chelsea nodded.

'I'd love to. Thanks, Sophie, that's the best Christmas present I could have received.'

'And she should know,' said Mark, ''cos she searched everywhere. She even had her hands down Santa's trou…'

'Stop!' Chelsea closed her eyes and raised a hand. 'I'm going to need therapy for a very long time after that.'

Mark looked at Sophie.

'See what I mean? I like your new assistant supervisor. Now, Chelsea, in your managerial capacity, can you arrange for a plate of free mince pies to be brought over, pronto?'

THE SIBLEY HALL MYSTERY

1

'*T*ake it easy, woman. If I wore dentures, I'd have lost them.' Ginger Salt reached for the door handle and clung on.

'If there's one thing I hate, it's drivers who slow down to go over cattle grids,' replied Joyce Brocklehurst over the sound of the engine as she changed gears and sped up even further.

'One thing? You have a long list, and my teeth could do with you getting over that particular dislike. I'm also wearing one of my older, less-supportive bras, so I need you to *take it easy.*'

'Not a problem I have.' Joyce glanced across at Ginger, who was now holding on to the edge of her seat with her other hand. 'But then I don't need the same level of support as some people.'

'I hope you're going to tone it down a bit when we get there.'

'Your friends will love me in all my glory.' Joyce paused. 'And yes, I am house trained, and I spend a lot of time around a Duke and Duchess so I know how to behave.' She shot through a puddle at 40mph, soaking a couple of hikers who were walking along the road. Ginger tried to remember the last time she'd been to church. She wasn't religious, but she was starting to wonder if she'd been a bit hasty in her conclusions about the existence of a god. Right now, she needed anything and everything on her side.

'Now tell me about this Milton chap – is he single?' Joyce asked.

'Milton is old enough to be your... well, maybe he is the right age, but he's not available. I can't believe you'd suggest such a thing; he was married to...'

'...one of your closest friends, I know. I'm joking.'

Ginger took a deep breath; she was beginning to wonder if maybe she should have done this on a different day. She and Joyce had a booking for dinner followed by a musical at the Buxton Opera House, but on the way they were visiting the home of some of Ginger's long-standing friends. She had altered a wedding dress and was dropping it off for the bride-to-be to try on.

'How did you meet Rosemary?' Joyce enquired.

'She knew my mum. They grew up on the same street. Mum was a bit older than her, but they became firm friends, and as I got older, Rosemary became my friend too.'

'How did someone who you make sound so perfect end up with this Milton? You describe him as a grumpy old git.'

'Family. Their parents were friends and they viewed it as a good match. Milton was handsome, a bit older, doing well in business and was what you might call *up and coming*. Rosemary was beautiful and the perfect hostess. I'm sure a lot of his business success came on the back of her ability to host a memorable dinner party and charm whoever Milton was trying to get money out of.'

'You make it sound like an arranged marriage.'

'It was in a way.'

'They weren't in love?'

'To misquote the fabulous Tina Turner, *what the 'eck has love got to do with it?*'

Joyce grunted in response. 'Maybe that was my mistake: I

thought I was in love each time I got married. I should have done like Milton and Rosemary and found someone who was good for business.'

'Rubbish! You might like to come across as tough as old boots, but you're the biggest romantic I've ever come across.'

'Keep that to yourself. How did Rosemary put up with him all those years if he was such a cold fish to her?'

'He wasn't, not after they'd been married a while. I guess they found a way of making it work – he started to appreciate everything she did behind the scenes and there's no escaping the fact that she was gorgeous. She also gave him three beautiful children. He was successful, made a name for himself, and he was quite a looker in his own way.

'As time went on, they became very happy together; at least, that's the impression Rosemary gave me. Milton was heartbroken when she died, reverted to his quiet ways. Once the eldest, Norton, was old enough to take over the family haulage business, Milton locked himself away, quite literally. Every afternoon, he goes into his study, locks the door and everyone knows not to disturb him.'

'What's he doing in there if he's handed the business over?'

'I don't think he has, not entirely. He likes to keep his hand in, goes over all the paperwork. Drives Norton nuts.'

Joyce had finally slowed down as she navigated a turning between two large stone pillars, a lion sitting regally on the top of each one, and ventured down the gravel driveway. Ginger relaxed for the first time on the journey, although she realised she was going to have to get used to Joyce's driving. Her friend would never change. If anything, the more Ginger protested, the worse Joyce's driving would get.

'How do you know all this?'

'Heather, the middle child. After her mother died, we got quite close. We usually have lunch once a month – she likes champagne as much as you do. I was one of the first people she told she was getting married, when she asked if I'd make a few alterations to Rosemary's wedding dress so she could wear it.'

'Nice idea.'

'She's a nice girl. I just wish her mum could be here for the wedding.'

As Joyce tucked her convertible BMW between a sleek black Audi and a white Mini Cooper, she looked up at Sibley Hall. She spent her days working in Charleton House, one of England's finest stately homes, so Ginger hadn't expected her to be particularly blown away, but she was pleased to see her friend taking the time to examine the handsome Palladian country house. Ginger wasn't the kind to be swayed by ostentatious displays of wealth either, but Rosemary had been key to the success of her family and Ginger was proud of her.

A building designed to impress and home to various dukes, a reverend and an industrialist, the house had been built in 1750. It had also been a hotel until Milton Tasker had purchased it to provide a family home for his new bride and their future children. The main building held five elegant reception rooms, six bedrooms, two studies, numerous bathrooms, a games room, and more. The older, smaller north wing held further guest rooms and staff accommodation, which had become a large nursery. Much of the house had been mothballed as Milton now lived alone, but Heather had recently revealed that he had agreed to her and her fiancé moving in after the wedding.

The large black door was flung open and a slim woman with blonde hair bounded down the steps before wrapping her arms around Ginger's neck.

'Ginny, I've missed you.'

'It's only been a month, Heather,' Ginger muttered through a mouthful of the younger woman's hair.

'I know, but I need you to tell everyone to calm down and

stop making such a fuss about the wedding. Oh, hello...' Heather stepped back, a little surprised to see Joyce, but the smile quickly returned to her face as she reached out to shake the older woman's hand. 'I like your... is it a coat?'

'Joyce, meet Heather. Heather, meet Joyce Brocklehurst... and her amazing Technicolor dream coat.' Joyce briefly glanced at her friend with a scowl, but beamed at Heather who was still admiring the multicoloured knee-length striped summer coat. Joyce had paired it with a lime-green t-shirt, white jeans, and bright-yellow heeled brogues. Ginger had to admit she secretly admired the way Joyce didn't worry about clashing colours; she just threw them all on in the hope some of them would go well together. At least, that was Ginger's view; Joyce would no doubt argue that it was a well-considered style choice each and every time.

Ginger herself had opted for a long, flowing cream linen top, which hid the fact that she could no longer fasten her rather old linen trousers properly. The problem stemmed from her unwillingness to give up desserts, and the older she got, the more she subscribed to the 'do whatever makes you happy' approach to life.

'Well, come in out of the rain, both of you,' said Heather. 'I've asked Theresa to bring us some drinks.' Ginger pulled a large bag off the back seat of the car and Heather clapped her hands. 'I'm so excited to see the dress, but drinks and gossip first.'

A bottle of Moët & Chandon was cooling in an ice bucket. Ginger watched as Joyce gave it an approving glance before scanning the room. Flocked wallpaper in pistachio green created a delicate background for a heavy marble fireplace. The pale pink sofa and armchairs gathered around the fireplace made the room look rather dated, the ornate gold picture frames and excess of side tables and cabinets placing the room firmly in 'old money stately home' territory, which Ginger knew had been heavily cultivated. There was the distinct smell of lemon furniture polish.

Heather stepped into the role of hostess as easily as her mother had. 'Please sit. Ah, glasses, yes. I hadn't realised that Ginger was bringing anyone, but I'm very glad she has. I'll call... oh, Theresa, thank you.' A woman in black trousers and a fitted cream blouse walked in, carrying a single champagne glass on a small tray.

'I saw your guests arrive.'

Ginger gave her a quick hug. 'Theresa, good to see you. You're looking well. Hope this one's not giving you the run around.' Ginger nodded towards Heather. Theresa laughed fondly.

'Far from it; trying to do too much, as ever.' With this, Ginger noticed the shadows under Heather's eyes for the first time. They were harder to spot when she was laughing and smiling, but they were there.

As Theresa left, a tall man with dark hair and intense dark eyes strode in, immediately making a beeline for Ginger and giving her an affectionate hug.

'Norton, this is a nice bonus,' said Ginger. 'I didn't expect you to be here. Meet Joyce.'

The oldest of the three Tasker children gave her a brief wave. 'Welcome. When Heather told me you were coming, Ginger, I had to hang around and see you. Rufus is about too, he'll want to say hello. I think he rather needs a friendly face.'

'Something up?' Ginger asked with concern.

'Broken heart. It turns out that Jane had someone else on the side. He didn't have a clue and was torn up by it.'

Ginger screwed up her face. 'Ouch. That's a shame, I really thought she was the one. Well, tell him I've arrived.'

'Will do. I'll be back later to say a proper hello; now, I'll leave you girls to talk shoes and veils. Good to meet you, Joyce.'

Norton strode out of the room with confidence evident in his posture. Heather filled the three glasses with Ginger watching closely, trying to work out if the young woman was as relaxed about the upcoming nuptials as she had claimed each time they chatted. It was to those upcoming nuptials that Ginger made the toast, but as each of them raised a glass to their lips, a loud bang shattered the moment.

Ginger immediately realised two things. Firstly, that was most definitely a gun shot, and secondly, while she and Heather had spilt their drinks, Joyce had not lost a drop. She merely raised her perfectly tweezered eyebrows at Ginger over the top of her glass.

2

*I*t wasn't that Joyce was used to the sound of a gun being fired, although she knew immediately that was what it was. It was more that she valued a glass of good champagne, and she was going to need it to get through what no longer promised to be a relaxing day of drinks, dinner and a trip to the theatre.

'Bloody Nora!' cried Ginger, placing her sloshing glass on the table. 'Where did that come from?'

'Upstairs, I think.' Heather had turned pale. She ran towards the door, narrowly avoiding a collision with Norton in the hallway. 'Did you hear that?' she asked him.

'Of course I bloody did. Come on,' he replied. Joyce followed on behind as they all ran up the wide staircase, Ginger barrelling her way up with surprising speed. All the dark wood, ornate carving and deeply patterned red carpets gave it a masculine feel and Joyce felt very much as though she was entering another world, one in which they would find Poirot standing over the victim of the gunshot.

As they turned the corner, Joyce spotted a blond-haired man

up ahead. He had just reached a doorway and was hammering on the closed door.

'Father, open up! Father, are you alright?' He bent down to peer through the keyhole. 'Can't see a damned thing, the key's in the lock.' He started his hammering again.

'I'll try the other way.' Heather ran through a door which Joyce could see led to a second study. Peering into the room, she saw the young woman trying to open a door in the far corner, adjoining the room they wanted to get into. After rattling the handle a few times, she was joined by Norton who threw his weight against it. It didn't budge.

'Father, for God's sake, open up!'

Ginger looked on, worry etched across her face. Joyce stepped aside to make way for the blond man.

'I'll go and get a ladder, take a look from outside.'

'Wait, Rufus, I'll come with you.'

'NO!' he shouted back at Norton before lowering his voice. 'You wait here with Heather, I might need you up top.'

Ginger was rooting around on the desk, eventually finding a letter opener and poking it into the lock. Joyce looked around the room, wondering if there was something they could use as a battering ram. There was nothing. She patted her head, trying to remember if she'd used a hairpin that would work better on the lock than the letter opener, but the only thing supporting today's gravity-defying hairstyle was half a can of hairspray.

Before she had a chance to think of anything else, the sound of a metal ladder banging against the wall of the house distracted them all. Ginger opened the window and leaned out.

'Be careful, Rufus.'

'Quick, we still can't get in,' called Heather over her shoulder. Joyce stood back, watching from a distance, almost falling into a wheelchair that had been tucked into a corner.

'DAD!' shouted Rufus as he tried to force the window. An exclamation of 'Oh dammit' was followed by the sound of shattering glass. Joyce wanted to get a better view and squeezed between Ginger and Heather to lean out of the study window. Rufus had pulled the sleeve of his jumper over his hand to protect it and was now carefully punching out bits of glass until he was able to haul himself through the window.

The thud of Rufus landing on the floor was followed by the sound of the door being unlocked. Heather ripped it open. Before them, Milton Tasker was slumped on his desk. Joyce didn't need to be told that within minutes of their arrival, the master of the house had been shot dead.

$\mathcal{I}$t had taken Ginger raising her voice to get everyone calmed down. Now the police had been called, she made her way back downstairs with Joyce, who had taken the executive decision that what they both needed was a drink. Ginger hadn't argued. Heather came with them, leaving her brothers sitting in the adjoining study, determined not to leave their father alone until the authorities arrived.

'It was definitely a gunshot?' Joyce asked Ginger, keeping an eye on Heather and feeling that *'Did you see a bullet hole?'* was a little insensitive. Ginger, who had got closer to the body than Joyce, nodded gravely.

'Definitely. I don't see how, though. Both doors were locked from the inside, and there isn't anything directly opposite the window: no building, no hill. I don't understand.'

'Is there a tree opposite that someone could have climbed?'

'No,' answered Heather, her face having taken on a permanently startled expression. 'Father liked that room precisely because of the clear view across the valley. No obstructions. Nothing that anyone could have climbed.'

Ginger laid a hand on her young friend's arm. 'Shall we change the conversation?'

'No, no, it doesn't make sense. I don't know who would have wanted to kill him, let alone how.'

'Are you sure about that?' Both women turned to face Joyce, who was sitting in a leather armchair, feeling thoughtful and a little regal. 'Heather, dear, I'm sorry to ask this at such a sensitive time, but are you certain that you can't think of anyone who might have wanted to kill your father? No business acquaintances he'd annoyed, local landowners disputing boundaries? Had he talked about changing his will?'

'Joyce!' Ginger's eyes were practically popping out. 'What do you think this is? An Agatha Christie novel? He wasn't the lord of the manor arguing with his tenant farmers.'

'Perhaps not, but someone was unhappy. Unless it was suicide.'

'It's okay, Ginny, she's only trying to help.' Heather took a moment, drained the glass of the champagne that Joyce had insisted she drink, and then turned to face her. 'He hadn't been very involved in the business for a couple of years. He'd handed all of that over to Norton. He still played a part, went over the paperwork, sat on the board, had a say in the big decisions, but it was mainly in Norton's hands now. I'm not aware of any disputes; the business is doing well, the money is coming in, the bills are being paid. As far as I know, it's a very viable business. Norton has plans to expand; he's full of ideas.'

'Away from the business?'

'He didn't have much of a life outside of work. After Mother died, he became a bit of a recluse; I can't remember the last time he left the estate. He goes for his walks, spends his afternoons locked in the study, and then comes out for dinner.'

'And your mother died...?'

'Nine years ago.'

'And it can't have been suicide, there was no gun in the room,' said Ginger, staring ahead, her eyes unfocused.

'No, he'd never do that. It wouldn't be his style,' Heather confirmed.

Joyce looked across at Ginger. There was a strange expression on her face. Joyce hadn't known her friend for very long, but she was starting to recognise a few things about her. This was the expression Ginger made when she was faced with a problem: when her car had broken down, again; when the washing machine door had jammed shut; when the front had fallen off Joyce's wardrobe. Each time, Ginger had pondered the situation, and eventually concluded that while she had no clue how to fix things immediately, she would blooming well work it out.

Joyce spent a lot of time with another amateur sleuth back at Charleton House and Ginger was clearly thinking along the same lines. If Ginger was keen to work this latest puzzle out, Joyce was also up for the challenge.

4

'*M*r Tasker, I'm Detective Sergeant Colette Harnby.' Ginger knew Joyce would have recognised the voice even if they hadn't heard the woman introduce herself to Rufus, the youngest of the three siblings. DS Harnby had worked on a number of cases at Charleton House, one of which Ginger had become embroiled in, marking the beginning of her and Joyce's friendship. The women were watching from the top of the stairs, tucked just out of sight. The forensics team in their white suits were already in the study and the detective was now talking to the family members. She would get to Joyce and Ginger soon enough.

'Come on, let's stay out of her way and go and talk to Theresa.'

Ginger led them down the stairs, along corridors with expensive-looking artwork and warm yellow lighting to a large kitchen. She had lost track of the hours she had spent in here with Rosemary, usually making themselves cheese plates to go with expensive bottles of wine, happy to risk the wrath of Milton if they had chosen one of his favourite reds. They had sat together at the large rustic table into the early hours of the morning, dissecting the behaviour of guests at the party that had just come to an end. Rosemary had used Ginger as a sounding board before presenting Milton with a business idea or shared her concerns when the children were going through their difficult teenage years, so it felt utterly right to Ginger that she was going to try to work out what had happened. After all, she was the one Rosemary would have turned to had she still been alive.

The housekeeper was slowly stirring a big pot of soup. The aroma of chicken and rosemary filled the air. The large kitchen had high ceilings and a clear view of a walled garden, its terra-cotta tiles echoing under Joyce's heels. An enormous wooden table, worn smooth over the years, dominated the centre of the room. Despite the crisp white walls and perfectly displayed utensils and pans, the kitchen looked well used, not like a showpiece.

'I can't imagine anyone will want much to eat, but this is something that they can come and get any time. I'll make them anything they want, but this way...' Theresa sniffed and patted the corner of her eye with a tissue that looked about ready to fall apart.

'It smells great. Why don't you come and sit down?' Ginger pulled out the stool next to her at the table. After blowing her nose, Theresa joined her. She'd clearly been crying, a lot. 'You must have seen a lot of Milton, maybe more than some of the family?'

Theresa nodded. 'Every day I was at work. I did most of the cooking for him, a lot of the cleaning.'

'Did he seem worried about anything? Did he say anything to you? Maybe you overheard something?'

'You mean about someone who might have wanted to kill him? No, nothing.' Theresa sniffed again, a long snotty sound. Ginger saw Joyce cringe at the noise.

'Did you hear any arguments? On the phone, maybe, if he didn't go out much.'

'No, nothing has changed around here for a long time. The family would come and go, more so as the wedding gets closer.

He'd lock himself away, and then come out for dinner.' This mirrored everything Heather had told them.

'It sounds like a very quiet life.'

Ginger knew that things had changed after Rosemary had died. She was organising dinner parties right up until the end, even designing the seating plan from her bed if necessary. Ginger had often come to help out, to be Rosemary's ears and eyes during the evening once her friend could no longer get out of bed to attend the dinners that she had arranged.

'I suppose so, although it didn't really feel that way, with the children and grandchildren coming over, and he was still working with Norton.'

Joyce stepped away from the wall. She towered over the table as she took a turn at asking questions.

'I thought that the business had been passed on to Norton.'

'It had, largely. Milton still wanted to check over everything, and he had some very strong views on how parts of the business should be run.'

'Did the two of them ever argue?'

'Sometimes, yes. I tried not to pay any attention, but it could get quite heated. That was just their way, though; it would all be fine by the time I served dinner, as though nothing had happened.'

'Did they argue recently?' Joyce had perched herself on the edge of the table. If it wasn't for the multi-coloured outfit, she could have looked quite threatening. As it was, she looked more like a gay pride flag than a hard-nosed private detective playing the bad cop role, but still, Ginger decided she would have a word with her about body language and the risk of intimidating potential witnesses.

Theresa sniffed again, and then started to cry. Ginger handed her a tissue from the sleeve of her blouse, patted Theresa on the shoulder and stood up.

'We'll leave you to it. Joyce, shall we…?'

'Ginny, here you are.' Rufus blocked their exit. Ginger stood and gave him a hug. He looked like the proverbial rabbit in the headlights.

'Have a seat. My God, that must have been awful for you, seeing your father like that.' She steered him towards a stool at the table. 'Theresa, you must have something stronger than soup down here. Whisky? Brandy?'

'I'm alright, Ginny.'

'I doubt that.' Rufus had maintained the same charm he'd possessed as a child. He was always the beautiful blond-haired boy who had wrapped the adults around his finger. Theresa placed a glass of whisky in front of him and Ginger gave her a look that was immediately understood. A second glass appeared. Joyce shook her head when Theresa offered her one. Ginger watched the housekeeper out of the corner of her eye as she quietly slipped out of the room.

'I heard about Jane. She better hope that I don't run into her...'

Rufus's shoulders slumped and Ginger put an arm around them. She was still standing so her hug left him squished against her ample bosom. It didn't matter that he was no longer a six-year-old with a grazed knee; this was precisely what ample bosoms were made for. She took a gulp of whisky, simultaneously giving his shoulders another squeeze.

'I'll be alright,' he mumbled again. 'None of it feels very real at the moment.' He sat up, pulling himself out of Ginger's clutches, and looked over at Joyce. 'This is quite the introduction to the family. I can't imagine you'll want to come back any time soon.'

'Oh, I don't know. It's certainly not dull around here, and if Ginger and I can help in any way, then it will have been the perfect time for us to visit.'

'Well, the police are here now, so I suppose we all just need to wait and follow their instructions.' He sipped the whisky as he spoke. 'I still don't understand how it happened. The windows were completely secure. Father would never have killed himself, but there wasn't anyone else.'

'And no gun,' Ginger reminded him.

'Was there a hole in the glass where the bullet went through?' Joyce had joined them at the table. Ginger gave her a warning look that she hoped would be correctly interpreted as *go easy on him.*

'The glass was broken, but I didn't pay much attention to it. I was just trying to figure out how to get in.'

'But it could have been a bullet hole?'

'I guess so. But I don't see where the gun could have been fired from.'

'Has there been any work done on the house recently?' Joyce asked him.

'Not for a while, why?'

'I was wondering about scaffolding or something like a cherry picker with one of those platforms that gets raised.'

Rufus shook his head. 'No, nothing like that.' His phone buzzed and he took it out of his back pocket. 'It's Norton, the police want to talk to me.' He stood up and gave Ginger another hug. 'Don't go anywhere, I want more time with you.'

The two women watched him leave.

'I do worry about him. He was always the more sensitive of the two boys. He once told me that he thought Jane might be the one he would marry. If she was playing away, then he'll be devastated. I must have a proper chat with him; I think he'll be comfortable talking to me now his mother isn't around. Come on, let's find somewhere more comfortable.'

Ginger plonked her empty glass heavily on the table and led the way.

5

'*H*ow long has she been with the family?' Joyce had made herself comfortable in a window seat and put her legs up on the cushions. It had stopped raining, but the sky was still a pale grey and the atmosphere was muggy. *Sodding British summer*, she grumbled to herself. But this was a cosy, private nook to hide themselves away in and there was a nice view over the grounds.

'Theresa? She arrived not long before Rosemary died, an extra pair of hands once Rosemary really started to struggle. Then when the previous housekeeper left a couple of years later, Theresa stayed on. She fitted in perfectly and is a very good cook.'

'I thought she was a bit over the top.'

'In what way? I've always been impressed by how much Theresa can operate in the background and not get underfoot. Drinks appear as if by magic, a wonderful spread of food is offered just as you are starting to feel hungry. But not today. Today, I must admit her heart isn't in it.'

'She had the face of someone who had been crying for the last couple of hours.'

'Her employer has just been shot dead, what do you expect?'

'Yes, I get that, but it was more than shock or upset. You'd think one of her own family had just died.'

'Maybe they feel like family after all these years.'

'I've worked for the Duke and Duchess of Ravensbury for a lot longer than Theresa has been here and you won't see me sobbing for hours at a time when one of them shuffles off.'

'That's because your empathy went missing in action years ago.' Joyce looked at her quizzically. Ginger answered her unspoken question. 'I know this because you use phrases like *shuffles off.*'

'Well, I think there's more to it than that.'

'More to what than what?'

Ginger turned as Heather walked towards them. 'Heather, are you alright? Have the police seen you?'

Joyce swung her feet off the cushions and made room for Heather to sit.

'Not yet, they're with Rufus. What do you think there's more to, Joyce?' Heather looked tired and Joyce could see she had been crying too, but she looked more composed than the housekeeper.

'Theresa. What was her relationship with your father like?'

'Ha! Did you spot it too?' Heather smiled sadly. 'She's always had the hots for Father, although that sounds rather an odd thing to say at his age. Oh God, I'd forgotten about that! She must be devastated; have you seen her?'

Joyce nodded. 'She was a bit of a mess.'

'I'll go and check on her in a minute. It'll give me something to do, stop *me* turning into a mess.'

Ginger looked thoughtful. 'In all the times I have visited the house over the last few years – kindly invited by you, Heather, but warmly welcomed by everyone – Theresa never seemed to change. She has always been efficient, attentive. I imagined she would die on the job at a grand old age, but I never spotted an unprofessional level of interest in Milton.'

'Did your father know?' asked Joyce.

'Yes, I believe he did. Last year, there was a period where Theresa didn't seem her usual self. She said she was okay, just feeling a bit under the weather, but it went on for a while. I spoke to Father about it and he said something about her getting some silly notions in her head. After a while, things went back to normal and I didn't think about it again.

'Last Christmas, Father had a couple more glasses of sherry than usual. We were talking about the wedding and I asked him if he'd ever remarry again. He said no, despite an offer. The way he said it, I thought it was the drink talking and just laughed, but Theresa was in the room. She left pretty quickly, looking like she was about to cry. It was only a couple of days later that I put two and two together. I might actually have got it wrong, but I don't think so.

'I should go and see if she's okay. Can I fetch you anything from the kitchen?'

The two women shook their heads and watched Heather walk off down the corridor. Joyce swung her feet back up onto the window seat.

'So far, we have the elder son arguing with Milton over business and a lovelorn housekeeper. But we're forgetting one vital thing which makes the subject of possible suspects completely pointless.'

'And that is?'

'How on earth did they do it? The only two doors into the room were locked from the inside and the keys were still in place. Milton was sat facing the window and you told me the injury was on the front of his body, so the obvious direction of the bullet is from the window, but there is nothing outside that would have made that possible. If we worked out how the killer did it, that might give away their identity.'

Ginger pushed Joyce's feet to the back of the seat and sat

down next to her. 'Okay, clever clogs, what ideas have you got? Because I assume you have some.'

'I have a couple of ideas. Do you know how to get onto the roof?'

'Not only do I know, I have spent a number of New Year's Eves out there, drunk a fair bit of wine there over the years and even indulged in a couple of joints in the open air when Rosemary suggested we see what all the fuss was about. And yes, I can claim that I did indeed inhale. Follow me. Now it's stopped raining, if anyone looks up, they'll just assume you're a rainbow.'

'Fingers crossed we'll find a pot of gold up there,' replied Joyce, swirling her coat around her. 'Or at the very least, a clue as to how the killer was able to shoot Milton.'

6

'Right then, we're looking for anything that indicates a rope was used. Look out for signs of rubbing against the stonework, strands, or even better, a rope curled up in the corner covered in DNA and a gun sat right in the middle of it.'

Joyce scanned the rooftop, convinced this was a sensible place to start. 'One way the killer could have done this is to lower themselves down, shoot Milton through the window, and then quickly pull themselves back up here. We were all so busy trying to get into the study that we would never have noticed someone coming back down off the roof and making a quick getaway, or they could have hidden away and escaped later. They might even still be here – well, hopefully not up here precisely, otherwise this might not go well, but somewhere in the house.'

She glanced over at Ginger, who was leaning as far over the edge as she possibly could and didn't seem to be paying much attention to what she was saying. Ginger clearly wasn't afraid of heights.

'Careful, girl. You spotted anything?' Joyce said, impressed by her friend's fearlessness.

'No, but I don't think we're going to find anything up here.' Joyce joined her at the edge and put a hand on her shoulder. The stone parapet only reached their knees and Ginger's position was precarious. 'I reckon we're above the study window. Now if I lean over a bit more...'

Joyce grabbed the waistband of her trousers, trying not to snap a lime-green nail in the process or think about the drop below. As she clung on to her friend, she watched two police officers in uniform chatting next to a car. She looked down at her own car and saw that a passing bird had taken a successful aim at the roof. She'd need to go to a carwash sooner rather than later.

'...I can't see a thing. They would have had to be an expert abseiler to do this without putting their foot through the window. Otherwise, it would be just too tricky to pull off.' Ginger leaned forward a bit more and Joyce tightened her grip on the fabric in her hand.

'Oi, go careful back there. I've never been a fan of G-strings,' Ginger called over her shoulder.

Detective Sergeant Harnby stepped out of the house and into view on the driveway, interrupting a call on her phone to glare at the two women on the roof.

'Bugger, come on.' Joyce hauled her friend back. 'It's not impossible, though?'

Ginger had sat on an orange plastic chair with rusty metal legs. She looked rather hot and was now trying to battle her unruly grey hair back into place.

'Right. But they would have had to have practised it, which means that they are either family, or they work here.' She looked out across the roof to the view beyond. 'Family. Bleeding Nora, why would one of the family do it? I'm glad Rosemary's not here to see all of this. Milton could be hard work, but he didn't deserve this, and I can't imagine one of the children doing it. I've always liked Theresa, but I'm far more comfortable with the idea of it being her.'

'They're not children, though, are they? Not anymore.' This was the first time Joyce had really registered how hard this would be for her friend. She'd watched the affection with which the Taskers had welcomed Ginger into the house; she was clearly important to them, and they to her. 'Are you sure you're comfortable doing this? We could just leave it to the police and go and get very drunk.'

'Not a chance, I want to know what happened. Come on, we're not going to find anything up here.'

Joyce agreed. She let Ginger lead the way, wrapped up in her own thoughts.

As they walked from narrow corridors with old wooden floors into bright spaces with luxurious carpets, Joyce spotted a photograph, taken during the Second World War, of a regiment in ceremonial dress.

'Ginger, guns.'

'What about them?'

'Train of thought. That picture reminded me we need to know more about the murder weapon. I guess the family was into shooting of some kind?'

'Occasionally, Milton used to do it as a young man, but the business took over.'

'And the children?'

'They all did it at one time or another. I think Milton was trying to get in with a certain kind of set – he'd play golf or go to shoots. Some of it was business, some just time with friends. Early on, he encouraged the children to shoot, but it wasn't really his thing, and Rosemary didn't like it.'

'So they all know how to use a gun?'

'Yes. They'd be rusty, but yes.'

'And there are guns here at the house?'

'The gun safe is in the basement. I know where the key is. Come on.' Ginger led the way, Joyce once again impressed at her determination and ability to stop any emotional response over-whelming her. She wondered if she could expect an outpouring of grief and tears when this was all over. Joyce wasn't very good in those situations; she never knew what to say and was very much of the 'pull yourself together' school of thinking. Fortunately, Ginger seemed to be made of pretty stern stuff and would prob-ably need a bottle of whisky and deep and meaningful conversa-tions until the early hours. Both of these Joyce could do, so long as she wasn't required to reveal her own deep and meaningfuls.

She was still thinking about how Ginger would react, when they walked through a door off the side of a dark basement corridor and found themselves face to face with Detective Sergeant Harnby and a uniformed officer. Not a single hair of Harnby's shoulder-length bob was out of place, and her entire outfit looked, as it always did, as if it had just come freshly pressed from the dry cleaners. Joyce found her style a little too tidy, even for a police officer.

Harnby looked at them both with an expression of calm expectancy.

'I wondered when I was going to get to speak to you two. This place isn't that big.'

'We were just waiting for the call,' Joyce replied reassuringly. 'Very keen to assist, but we knew you'd be talking to the family so we were trying to stay out of your hair.'

'And you have chosen to do that up on the roof and down here in the basement because…?'

Joyce could see the small gun safe behind DS Harnby. The door was open and she was trying to see the contents. Ginger stepped in to explain, or rather make an excuse.

'I was just giving Joyce the grand tour. As she works up at Charleton House, I thought she might be interested in seeing behind the scenes of Sibley Hall. Not as impressive, of course, but still very interesting.'

'Fascinating,' added Joyce, nodding furiously. Ginger seemed to be trying to indicate something to her.

'Over here, for example,' Ginger continued, pointing to a row of small holes in the wall roughly at head height. 'This room used to be the housekeeper's office and these holes are where a row of small bells was attached so the family could ring and get the servants' attention.' As Harnby turned to see what Ginger was pointing at, Joyce took a couple of steps to the side so she had a clear view of the safe. Three rifles and two handguns, both of which looked very old. There was no sign of anything being out of place or missing. She took a good long look, and then stepped back.

'It really is fascinating, Ginger, I'm sure there's a lot more you can show me. We ought to leave DS Harnby and this fine young man to continue with their work.'

'Absolutely, right you are.'

'I still need to interview you both so don't go anywhere. And stay away from the study.'

'I'm curious,' Ginger opened the door as she spoke to the detective, 'has Milton been taken away?'

'He has. I believe you are a friend of the family. I'm very sorry.'

'Thank you, sergeant. We'll be here whenever you want to talk to us.'

7

'We still don't know how they did it.' Ginger was running through everything in her mind. How did this family, one that she had known for forty years, go from being far from perfect but reasonably normal to the centre of a murder investigation? A very bizarre murder at that. 'We have no idea how the killer got in and out and we don't know where the murder weapon has gone.'

'Yes, we do.' Joyce made it sound like Ginger was missing something very obvious.

'The guns were all there, you said so yourself.'

'Yes, they were, and when Harnby sends them off for testing, I bet that they're going to find that one of them has been fired recently. I'm guessing one of the antique guns was used. At least, they looked like antiques.'

'A Smith & Wesson and a Colt. They were Milton's grandfather's. He talked about starting a collection, but Rosemary put her foot down.'

'Good woman. Bloody awful things. Why would you want to be reminded of the dreadful things guns can do?'

'You mean kill someone?'

'That's exactly what I mean!' declared Joyce.

'But if one of those guns is the murder weapon, then that means that a member of the family did it. After all, they know where the safe is and where the key is kept. I've tried imagining one of them as capable of this, but I just don't see it.'

'And you don't have to. We already know that Theresa has been spurned by Milton – that gives her a pretty solid motive. Apart from the broken heart, assuming her feelings are genuine, she's missed out on all this.' Joyce waved her arms around, indicating their surroundings. 'If Milton had married her, then she'd presumably have inherited everything, or a big chunk of it.'

'And then there's Norton,' Ginger added reluctantly. 'Theresa said there had been arguments about the business.'

'Tell me about Rufus, you haven't said much about him.'

Ginger sighed, picturing the child who used to sit on her shoulders and insist she run around the garden; who loved her homemade chocolate cake and would fall asleep in her lap after long, hot summer days.

'Rufus was a sweetheart, he still is. I wasn't at all surprised when he didn't follow his father into the haulage business. While Norton was playing with toy trucks, Rufus wanted to spend time with the adults. Happy to just sit and listen, he probably heard all sorts of secrets and admissions of indiscretion. He was too young to know what it all meant, of course. He went to university in Sheffield, not wanting to be too far from home, then became a teacher. Very close to his mother, he was devastated when she died.'

'And his father, did they get on?'

Ginger thought for a moment. She was very conscious of choosing her words carefully. She wasn't interested in hiding anything from Joyce, but she was talking about her friends and didn't want to say anything that could be misconstrued.

'Not in the early years. Milton had imagined both of his boys going into the family business, so he was bitterly disappointed when Rufus made it clear he wasn't interested. It wasn't until the grandchildren of some of Milton's business associates ended up at Rufus's school, and then in his class, that Milton started to hear what a great job he was doing, what a difference he was making to those children. I think he then saw that he and Rufus actually had something in common.'

'Which was?'

'Passion. They both loved what they did, put their heart and soul into it. It turned out they weren't so different after all. They became much closer after that, and Rufus even took a sabbatical from teaching to support his father after Rosemary died.'

'Come on.' Joyce stood.

'Where are we going?'

'DS Harnby said that they'd moved Milton. Chances are they've done with the study. We should go and take a look.'

Ginger liked the idea. A picture of the three children in their youth was getting stuck in her brain and she needed a distraction. The rebel in her savoured the prospect of sneaking a look into the very room DS Harnby had told them to steer clear of.

'What should you go and take a look at?' As if conjured by Ginger's thoughts, the steady, calm voice of DS Harnby made them both jump. Ginger was first to recover.

'We're going to see how things are with Heather and her brothers. If you've finished with them all, then there might be errands Joyce and I can run. We could give Theresa a break and make them something to eat – after all, it's almost dinner time. I'll do whatever I can to help them.'

'And you?' DS Harnby looked over at Joyce.

'Think of me as Cagney to her Lacey.' Ginger scowled at her. Comparing them to a couple of detectives wasn't a great idea at this point.

'Well, Cagney, I'll start with you, if you don't mind. I'm sure that Lacey can look after herself while I chat to you.'

Joyce raised herself from the seat gracefully. Running a hand down the stripes of her coat, she straightened her shoulders and followed DS Harnby out of the room. At least, Ginger thought, she now knew where the sergeant would be and she'd make less noise on her own. She waited, giving them a couple of minutes to get a head start, before quietly making her way upstairs.

Milton's study was eerily quiet and Ginger didn't really want to step in too far. There was no sign that a man had been murdered in here earlier in the day. She had only been in the study a handful of times over the years and it looked exactly as she remembered it.

Walls of bookcases were filled with leather-bound books. A row of tall steel-grey metal filing cabinets lined one wall, a bottle of whisky and a single glass on the top of one. She was tempted to pour herself a drink, but then decided that was just a little bit creepy.

Joyce would no doubt tell her to start rifling through the cabinets, but it was all too overwhelming. Instead, she took a deep breath and decided to start with the drawers in the antique wooden desk. Trying not to think that this was where Milton took his last breath, she started on the left and worked her way down. Pens, paper, another bottle of whisky, a tube of hand lotion, a bottle of eye drops; nothing of interest. In the drawers on the right, it was much the same.

The window that Rufus had broken, and that presumably a bullet had already pierced, was now boarded up, blocking most of the view. Ginger went and stood by the window, looking out through one of the panels to the side. There were trees within sight line, but she couldn't see how they would be strong enough to take the weight of an adult without bending and swaying, and surely Rufus would have seen something unusual when he went to get a ladder. The rest of them had all had access to the window in the room next door and no one had spotted anything.

Ginger had a look at the doors next – rattled the handles, turned the keys in the locks back and forth. There was nothing unusual. The keys didn't stick; they didn't show any signs of being tampered with. She pulled and tugged at the bookcases – no hidden doors. Ginger examined the latches on the window, which remained locked just as they had been when Rufus had climbed the ladder and had to resort to breaking the window. She pulled up the rug, no hidden trap door. There were no cupboards, no boxes, nothing to conceal a killer; and even if one had been there, they would have had to get past six people, if you included Theresa.

Without thinking, she sat down in Milton's chair and stared ahead at nothing in particular, picturing the creature of habit who had been Milton sitting in this exact same spot, his back ramrod straight, his chair always in the same place. Had Milton been dead for hours and the killer been and gone before she and Joyce had even arrived? But that still didn't explain how they got out with the doors and catches on the windows locked, or the gunshot they'd all heard. Ginger was stumped, and it wasn't a feeling she enjoyed.

8

'There's something just not right about being interviewed by a police detective who is younger than my socks.' Joyce stepped confidently into the room.

'I take it they've concluded you're not the killer?'

'Not this time, but I wouldn't rule it out in the future.' Ginger smiled. Joyce's directness was welcome right now. 'Found anything of interest?'

Ginger gave a great big sigh. 'No, nothing at all. Nothing that could point us in the direction of the killer and nothing that would tell us how they did it. Mind you, the police will have taken anything useful.'

'You'd hope, but DS Harnby seems as stumped as us. She's not saying it directly, but I can tell she's clutching at straws. They're still keeping an open mind about how it happened, which translates as "it's not suicide". Or at least, there is enough of a question mark over that.'

'Good, so we're not wasting our time.' Ginger got up from Milton's chair and eased it back into the indentations in the carpet that showed it always rested in exactly the same spot. 'Mind you, we are in here. Come on.'

Joyce stood up from her position leaning against the door frame. 'Where are we going?'

'Next door. I want to think about what we saw.'

The two women made their way through the connecting door, closing it firmly behind them, and into the much lighter study. Ginger was running her fingers back and forth through her hair, even though she knew it made her look a little bit like a sheep who'd had a run-in with a barbed-wire fence. Joyce sat behind Rosemary's desk while Ginger paced up and down the room as she spoke.

'We came up the stairs with Heather and Norton, both of whom had been with us or near us when the shot went off. We saw Rufus trying to get in through the door off the corridor. So he was locked outside when the gun was fired. Heather and Norton then came in here to try the connecting door, with no luck, and Rufus went to get the ladder.'

By now, Ginger was standing by the window, looking out. She opened it up and leaned out.

'Will you stop doing that?'

Ginger ducked her head back in. 'Doing what?'

'Leaning out over great heights. One death is enough.'

'Give over, I was just seeing if it's close enough.'

'If what's close enough to what?'

Ginger closed the window and went to sit down on the armchair opposite the desk, but it was covered in boxes. She couldn't be bothered moving them so dropped down into the wheelchair that was tucked to one side of the window.

'Close enough to climb between the two windows.' Ginger thought about what she had just said. 'But then, this window was locked from the inside too, and it would take some time to get back in, and they would have had to run past us. It still doesn't work.' She looked at Joyce. 'Any ideas?'

'I'm wondering where Theresa was.'

'I'm here.' Theresa was standing in the doorway and Joyce yelped. Ginger threw her hand to her chest.

'Dear God, Theresa, don't do that to me. I don't need any more drama today.'

'I'm sorry, Ginger, I came to see if I could get either of you anything. You must be starving.'

'I am rather. Joyce?'

Her friend had a look of concentration and suspicion. She swivelled her chair round until she was facing Theresa, put her elbows on the desk and tented her fingers. Ginger noted that all that was missing was a long-haired white cat.

'I was just wondering, Theresa, where you were when the gun went off and everyone ran upstairs.'

'I was in the kitchen. I didn't hear the gunshot, but I did hear a lot of commotion and the sound of running, so I came to the bottom of the stairs. Rufus dashed past me and told me to call the police. He thought that Milton had been hurt, so that's what I did.' Ginger made a note to check with Rufus that he had indeed spoken to Theresa at that point. Joyce nodded slowly, and then swivelled her chair back to the desk. Ginger stood, knocking over some crutches, walking sticks and other evidence of Rosemary's deteriorating health. She bent over to pick them up.

'I offered to get rid of those; I didn't see any point in hanging on to them, but this room became a bit of a shrine to her.' Theresa nodded and added, 'Milton didn't allow the regular cleaner in here, same with his study. I was the only one allowed to come in and dust it.'

Ginger's phone rang. 'Hello... Yes, of course, where should I meet you?... I'll be right down... Now? I was just having a lie down in one of the bedrooms, I'll be two minutes.' She hung up quickly. 'DS Harnby. She's ready to talk to me.'

9

Once Ginger had left, Joyce looked towards the wheelchair and the other paraphernalia. Her eyes narrowed as she focused on a curious contraption and the seeds of an idea began to germinate in her brain, but Theresa hovering in the doorway was making her uncomfortable and she decided she might as well make use of the woman's presence. She had learnt a little about Norton and Rufus, but Heather was still a blank page to her, and she wondered if the close relationship between Heather and Ginger was colouring Ginger's view of her.

'I don't know the family as well as Ginger, and I was wondering about Heather. What can you tell me about her?'

'I'm not sure I should be talking about her like this. I've known them for years and they trust me; she might walk in.'

Joyce got up and closed the door. 'One problem solved. Look, we just want to know what happened, and you know Ginger too. Surely you trust her? We're not muck-raking; we're trying to find out who killed Milton, and I'm sure that's something you want to know too. I suspect he meant a lot to you.'

At that, Theresa gave her a look of uncertainty.

She's trying to work out if I know how she feels about him, Joyce thought.

'Shouldn't we leave this to the police?'

'They have systems and processes and rules to follow and they won't have an answer overnight. The quicker we can figure this out, the quicker his children can move on.'

'I suppose.' Theresa finally sat down. 'What do you want to know about Heather?'

'Did she get on with her father?'

'You don't beat around the bush, do you?'

'I'm not known for it, no.'

'They got on fine. She wasn't quite Daddy's little girl, but almost.

'Did she work for him?'

'No. She runs her own business, something to do with logistics and shipping documents. I don't understand it.'

'Did he want her to go into the family business?'

'Heavens, no! He was a bit old-fashioned like that. He was happy that she went and set up her own business, but he expected one of the boys to take on the family firm.'

Joyce wasn't sure exactly what she was digging for. A reason for Heather to want her father dead, of course, but that could have been almost anything.

'How did Milton feel about the man Heather is marrying?'

'He liked Elliot, a self-made man like himself. He took to him immediately.'

'So, there was no reason Milton might not have wanted the wedding to go ahead?'

'No. In fact, Milton was frustrated that Heather didn't want a bigger event. She insisted on keeping it small, said she didn't want to throw money away on one day. Understandable as she had to be careful about her spending, what with money being tight. Milton did offer to pay, but she wouldn't take any financial help from him. She was always very independent.'

There it was. That was the kind of thing Joyce was looking for.

'Heather has money problems? But she has her own business.'

'She does. It doesn't mean it's successful. I've seen her paying suppliers for the wedding with credit cards, so I presume she hasn't got all the money she needs to cover it.'

Joyce thought about her own credit card, which was generally nearing its limit. Retail therapy was her favourite kind.

'That doesn't necessarily mean she's got financial problems.'

'She has quite a few cards on the go. I don't think I've seen her use the same one twice.'

Joyce had to admit it didn't quite make sense. A wealthy family, a father who liked the groom to be and who had offered to help pay for the wedding, and Heather was spreading her expenditure over numerous credit cards. It was worth looking at. But again, Heather was with them when Milton was shot, although she could have employed someone else to do it, promised them some of her father's money if they did the job well. It was tenuous, but worth a few more questions.

However, Theresa was resolute. 'I don't want to say any more. There's no way that Heather would be involved, she's really a very sweet person. She was a rock for her father after Rosemary died, and she and her husband planned to move in here with him after the wedding. There has never been any talk of him moving out; she wanted to live with her father and raise a family in this house.'

Did she really? Joyce wondered. *Or did she want Sibley Hall to herself?*

'I should go and prepare some more food; the soup has all gone and… well, I don't know what else to do.'

Joyce smiled. 'Of course. The family are lucky to have you here.' She hoped she sounded sincere. She thought she meant it, although Theresa's feelings for Milton still bothered her.

· · ·

With Theresa gone, Joyce sat and pondered everything she had been told. The room was quiet, and what had happened next door made it feel cold and still. Joyce felt as though she was waiting, although she wasn't sure what for. Was she waiting to hear a noise? To see the ghost of Milton walk through the wall? Was Rosemary going to send her a message, telling her who the killer was? Was she waiting for the killer to come and confront her, putting an end to her and Ginger's investigation by adding their bodies to the pile?

Out of curiosity, and for want of any better ideas, Joyce walked over to the stack of boxes on the armchair and moved them to the desk. There was no harm in having a look. On top of the boxes was a white photograph album and Joyce instinctively knew this would be Milton and Rosemary's wedding album. It was entirely as she expected: beautiful photos of a beautiful couple. Milton looked a little wooden, like a man uncomfortable in front of the camera and probably thinking he could make better use of his time at the office. But if what Ginger had said was true, he had grown to love his wife deeply and they had made a great couple.

Tissue paper protected each image and it crinkled loudly as she turned the pages. The pictures portrayed a standard wedding, the kind about which Joyce was increasingly cynical. After more marriages than she cared to think about, Joyce was beginning to wonder if Mr Actually – Finally – Where the Hell Have You Been? – Right would ever come along, and if he did, whether it was really necessary to go through the trouble of yet another wedding.

Who was she kidding? If nothing else, a wedding was an excellent excuse for one heck of a shopping trip.

10

$\mathcal{J}$oyce decided to allow her curiosity to get the better of her and opened the top box. She could imagine Heather going through the boxes to find the wedding album as she planned her own, where she would be wearing her mother's dress. More photos, these in envelopes. Faded shots of a family growing up together; children having fun in a river, taking part in school plays, winning awards. If Joyce had had the time to go through them all in detail, she could have watched the Tasker family change and grow over the decades.

In the second box, there were mountains of postcards from all over the world. A whole bundle were from Norton, who appeared to have spent a couple of months travelling in Europe; the Eiffel Tower, the Colosseum, the Sistine Chapel, they were all there. He wasn't particularly effusive in his messages, but at least he had made the effort.

Letters from Heather when she was at university; Rufus's Boy Scout badges all bundled together and secured with a green ribbon. Joyce wasn't prone to bouts of sentimentality, but she knew the family meant a lot to Ginger. She felt a slight twinge of regret at what they were going through on her friend's behalf.

'Find anything interesting?' Heather walked in with a glass of something sparkling in each hand. 'Ginger will be up in a minute, the police have finished with her and she's just catching up with Norton. She said you'd appreciate this.'

'She's a good one, is Ginger. Thank you. How are you holding up?' Heather looked remarkably composed; a little too composed for Joyce's liking.

'I'm not sure.' She looked over at the door to Milton's study. 'I think I'm only holding it together because there are so many people in the house. As soon as you all leave, there's a strong chance I'll fall apart.'

'Your fiancé is…?'

'Getting a flight back from Tokyo. He was there for business, but left for the airport as soon as I called him.'

'Did he get on with your father?'

'Yes, very well. I occasionally joke that I'm not sure whether Elliot is marrying me or the family.' She joined Joyce at the desk and picked up a bundle of letters.

'Going through all of this must have brought back memories.'

Heather shook her head. 'I'm not one for heading back down Memory Lane; that's Rufus. All I wanted was a picture of Mother in the wedding dress so I could have it on display at the wedding. Rufus knew where the wedding album was, and then spent hours going through everything else as well. He's much more sentimental than me.'

Joyce pushed the boxes aside. 'Heather, I have a question for you.'

Heather lifted the last couple of boxes off the armchair and sat down. 'Ask away.'

Joyce had concluded that it was better if she asked some of the more prying questions. She wasn't close to this family and had nothing to lose, whereas Ginger might understandably be a little more reticent.

'Are you aware of the contents of your father's will?'

'I am; we all are.'

'And has it changed recently?'

'No. Father rewrote it after Mother died and it's not been touched since. Norton gets the business; I get the house and a little money; Rufus gets quite a lot of money. Why, do you think one of us did it for the inheritance?' Bizarrely, Heather looked as if she was enjoying this line of questioning, so Joyce decided to push her luck a bit further.

'How's your cash flow these days?'

Heather laughed, trying not to spit out her drink. Joyce knew that had been a little abrupt, but why change the habit of a lifetime?

'Very good, thank you. Do you need a loan?'

Joyce chose to ignore the sarcasm. 'If we put the matter of the will aside for a moment, I'm just wondering why someone like yourself is insisting on a small wedding and paying for everything with an array of credit cards, and why you haven't commissioned the latest designer to the stars to make your dress. Although I do understand the desire to wear your mother's dress – it is very beautiful – so I can give you a pass on that one. The others remain pertinent questions.'

'I brought the bottle,' declared Ginger as she walked through the door, confirming for Joyce that she'd done the right thing in becoming friends with the woman. 'Why are you both looking so serious, apart from the obvious? What did I just walk in on?'

'Joyce was enquiring as to my financial status and I was about to put her concerns to rest, thereby – I hope – allaying any suspicion that I might have murdered my father in order to get my hands on my inheritance at a schedule of my choosing rather than that of Mother Nature or God, whoever you think is in charge around here.'

Ginger gave her friend a hard look, but Joyce could tell that she was a little relieved that she had done the dirty work for her.

'I do wish you wouldn't sit there,' Joyce told her as Ginger returned to her seat in the wheelchair. 'It's like a rather depressing vision of the future.'

'Ah, don't worry, I'll get a powered one and jimmy it so I can go up to 30mph in it. We'll be Thelma and Louise with blue rinses.'

'Anyone tries to give me a blue rinse and I'll break their arm,' Joyce stated firmly. 'Anyway, we're rather off topic.'

'We are,' agreed Heather, 'and I'm keen to dispel this notion of me as a possible suspect. Elliot and I are having a small wedding because I will be his second wife and we felt it would be more dignified if we didn't make a great hullabaloo. I have been spreading the payments around credit cards for the simple reason that I am collecting points. Now I have enough to pay for the flights for the honeymoon. It might seem ridiculous that someone with the amount of money I have, and will now inherit, bothers with that sort of thing, but I'm good with money and – like pretty much anyone you care to mention, no matter what their financial situation – I enjoy a bargain. And yes, I am wearing Mother's dress for purely sentimental reasons. It's beautiful and no designer could create anything better.'

'Happy now?' Ginger asked Joyce, who briefly considered a sarcastic response before reminding herself, once again, of the difficult situation Ginger was in.

'Very. Glad to hear it, Heather; never been one for big weddings myself.'

'And how many times have you tested that out, dear?' This time, Joyce glared at her friend without feeling an ounce of guilt.

As Ginger ran them through her interview with the police, which had been as straightforward as her own, Joyce started digging in another box.

'Have they any idea at all?' she could hear Heather asking.

'They're never going to admit to it, but I think they're stumped, mainly by how it happened...'

Joyce was tuning in and out of the conversation. She had been pulled into a set of letters that Rosemary had received.

'Heather, did your mother go away for a while about thirty years ago?' Joyce interrupted Ginger and Heather, who were still mid-conversation, but that didn't matter now.

'Yes, we all did. Well, Mother and all the children. Father was in the middle of a big deal and he needed to be free of distraction, so Mother took us to a friend's house in the South of France. One of the reasons I remember it is that we were gone the whole summer; we were taken out of school a week early and returned a week after the autumn term had started. The boys were both ecstatic, but I enjoyed school so wasn't so pleased.'

'And you didn't go through these boxes, you say?'

'No, why?'

Joyce was deep in thought. She was getting somewhere, but that didn't answer the question of how Milton had been killed.

'Are you going to drink that?' Ginger asked. Joyce looked at her half-empty glass; it was unlike her to be distracted *away* from a drink. Distracted *by* a drink, yes. She snatched it up off the desk as Ginger reached out, pretending to grasp it with a long yellow grabber that had been stored with the wheelchair and other aids, teasing her.

'Feel free,' said Joyce, holding the glass out to her. 'You're going to need another drink. I know who killed Milton.'

11

Joyce wanted to be certain of her conclusions before she said anything to Ginger or the family. She knew she could be flippant about a lot of things, but this was different; this she had to be absolutely confident of.

She shooed a concerned-looking Ginger and Heather out of the study and re-read the letters. They were, of course, only one side of a conversation, Rosemary's written responses not being included in the bundle. In fact, it was clear that Rosemary wasn't writing as often as the other correspondent, who would beg for a response and then be incredibly grateful for any reply from her, no matter how brief.

Next, Joyce made her way outside, familiarising herself with the route from the study to the flowerbed below the window that Milton had presumably been shot through. After experimenting with a stapler from Rosemary's desk, making a phone call, and then draining her champagne glass, Joyce joined Ginger and the family in a large, comfortable sitting room where she had asked Ginger to gather them together. It was cavernous compared to most people's sitting rooms, of course, but it was comfortably furnished in worn sofas and armchairs that had seen better days.

This wasn't a room for drinks following a formal dinner; this was where the family gathered and relaxed.

There was to be no relaxing this evening, though.

'What the hell is this all about?' demanded Norton. 'I feel like we're participating in a ridiculous murder-mystery weekend. Well, this isn't fun, it isn't a party, this is our father.'

'Just let her speak,' suggested Ginger kindly. 'Despite resembling a colour palette for a child's nursery, my friend can be quite astute.' Joyce chose to ignore the dig and concentrate on the complimentary part of Ginger's statement.

Heather had taken a seat in the window and was playing with a gold chain on her wrist, turning it round and round. Rufus, partly hidden behind his fringe, was pouring himself a whisky and looking as though he was putting up with a tiresome teenager who would eventually grow out of making outrageous statements. He was no longer the hurt and shocked boy from the kitchen. Theresa hovered at the door.

'Oh, come in and sit down, you're putting me on edge,' Norton snapped at her. Theresa followed his instructions and sat awkwardly on a hard-backed chair.

Joyce took a deep breath and prepared herself. As she stood at the centre of the room, she thought momentarily of the power she had in her hands – assuming, of course, that she was right. She was about to make a complete plonker of herself if she was way off the mark and Ginger would probably never talk to her again. But her friend was looking at her with an encouraging, if nervous, expression, willing her on.

Another deep breath. 'Despite your recent loss, you're a very fortunate family. You have financial security, a beautiful family home; a wonderful mother who passed far too soon, but left you with many happy memories; a father who, despite being on the curmudgeonly side, loved you all. It seems to me that you have all been taught to work hard and be independent, while supporting one another emotionally and being extremely loyal.

'So when one of you discovered something that undermined all that, especially as it mirrored your own life, it all became too much. The anger festered and you planned to get your own back, to seek revenge on behalf of the mother you had loved so dearly.'

At that, Joyce could see Theresa visibly relax. The house-keeper clearly understood that she was no longer in the frame. In contrast, Ginger tensed. Joyce knew her friend had always been more comfortable with the idea of Theresa as the murderer, but she had just made it clear that it was a family member.

Joyce considered a long, dramatic pause, thought about slowly looking at the faces of each and every person in the room, then watching as the killer registered that they had been discovered. But that would be cruel. It was time to tell them what she had worked out and name the killer, not play with their emotions.

'Rufus, it took you a long time to win your father's support. A long time for him to understand just how much you had in common: that you were both passionate, dedicated men who were committed to their work. You went as far as taking a sabbatical from the job you love to help him through the months following your mother's death and do all of the jobs that inevitably come with bereavement.

'But you didn't quite finish everything you had wanted to do in that time. There were still things of your mother's that needed to be sorted through and you only got round to that recently. As a result, you knew exactly where to find your parents' photo album when Heather wanted an image of your mother in her wedding dress.

'As often happens when nostalgia takes hold, you started looking through the other boxes and you got pulled in. We've all done it when cleaning out an attic or under the stairs – you mean to grab just one thing, but hours later you're still sat on the floor, surrounded by old photographs and family papers.

'You found something else, though, something that made you angry. Something that made you doubt everything that your relationship with your father was built on. That stewed within you until you could contain it no more and you found a rather ingenious way to kill your father.

'What was it that bothered you so much? He'd had an affair, hadn't he? The summer your mother took you all to the South of France, she was getting away from him. She was trying to decide what to do, recover from the hurt, maybe even punish him a little. I read his letters begging her for forgiveness, telling her how she had changed his life, how he loved her and it wouldn't happen again. I don't know what she said in response, but clearly she decided to return, to forgive him.'

Rufus hadn't moved. The glass of whisky remained untouched in his hand. Norton was staring intently at him, looking ready to leap out of his chair and take his own revenge; Heather and Ginger kept their eyes on Joyce, the older woman looking disappointed rather than angry or upset.

'You *wanted* the house full of people, Rufus. After all, there would be more witnesses to this murder; more people to say, "*I don't understand... it's impossible... no one here could have done it.*" But it wasn't that hard. Using the grabber that your mother had picked things up with towards the end of her life, you held the gun out of the window. Leaning out as far as possible, you shot your father through the glass. It was tricky and you had one chance to get it right, but you managed it. I was able to use the grabber to pick up a champagne glass earlier, and operate the stapler on the desk, so I know it's possible. All you had to do was make sure the two grips of the device were secure, one against the grip of the gun and the other against the trigger.

'Once you'd fired the shot, you allowed the gun to fall into the flowerbed and quickly put the grabber back by the wheelchair. By the time we got upstairs, you had locked the window and were already outside your father's study, banging on the door, and of course, there was no way you could have entered and exited the room. Your father had, as usual, locked it from the inside. You were most insistent that you were the one to go and get the ladder to climb up and see what was happening through the window. That gave you a chance to retrieve the gun from the flowerbed below and created the perfect excuse as to why your footprints were all over the place. Breaking the window to get in destroyed more evidence: the hole the bullet had created.

'When you climbed through the window and opened the door, the gun was in your pocket. As we all responded to your father's death, you had the opportunity to slip away and return it to the safe in the basement.'

Joyce stopped. She was no psychologist and didn't want to say too much about what had driven Rufus to commit murder, beyond avenging his mother. She didn't need to say any more as Heather spoke.

'She forgave him, you know, Rufus. She told me about it just after she got sick. Elliot had done something stupid and I confided in her. She confided in me in return, told me what had happened, how angry she was, but also how she had put us first and, over time, forgiven him. The marriage only became stronger after that. Mother would never have wanted this.'

There was a moment's silence before Rufus's anger broke it.

'But he betrayed her, and he was always going on and on about loyalty. It turned out it meant nothing, they were all empty statements. He should never have done that to her. I owed it to her to make him pay.'

'So you shot him? In cold blood?' Heather's outraged expression changed to one of bewilderment. 'But I still don't understand. How could you be sure Father would be at his desk? He could have been bending down to take something out of a drawer...'

'Whisky, probably,' muttered Norton, his face still a mask of shock. Heather carried on as if he hadn't spoken.

'...or over at the filing cabinets.'

'The deep indentations on the carpet show exactly where he

always sat,' explained Joyce, her gaze steady on Rufus, 'so it was straightforward enough for you to work out where you had to aim. But yes, you had to make sure he would be there.'

'The phone!' exclaimed Norton, his previously baffled dark eyes suddenly focused.

'Of course,' said Heather, turning to face her younger brother. 'You phoned him. After all, who didn't know that Father always sat at his desk to take a call?'

'It would certainly clarify that grey area. Did you phone your father, Rufus?' asked Joyce.

'Why should I tell you?' sneered the blond-haired man.

'No matter,' replied Joyce nonchalantly. 'I'm sure the police will be able to find out if a call was made from your phone to your father's office moments before he was shot.' She regarded Rufus with keen eyes. The man was squirming in his seat. 'Ah, I see from your body language that that's exactly what they will find.'

Rufus was silent, staring moodily into space. It was Heather who broke the awkward quiet.

'But why after all this time, Rufus?' she asked. 'There was nothing to be gained, he was an old man.'

'He still needed to pay.'

'But it wasn't just him you were getting back at, was it? You were also angry at Jane. You'd been betrayed yourself. You know, I realise now that you offered to find the wedding album and went through the boxes the same day you told me that Jane had slept with someone else. I guess the two things became indistinguishable to you.'

Norton suddenly looked up. 'You haven't killed her too, have you? There isn't a dead body somewhere that we need to tell the police about, is there?'

That was something Joyce hadn't considered.

'No, don't be an idiot,' Rufus shouted at his brother, and then turned to Joyce. 'I don't even know who you are, you interfering old...'

'Rufus, less of that!' Ginger stood, the look of an angry schoolmarm on her face. 'Hard though this is for me to take in, what you have committed is murder. You must have done your preparations, measured all the angles so that you'd know exactly where the gun had to be before you operated the grabber and pulled the trigger remotely.' Ginger fell silent for a few moments before making a suggestion in a choked voice. 'I think it's time we called the police.'

'No need.' DS Harnby stepped into the room. 'I'll take it from here. Thank you, Joyce.' She stood beside Joyce and whispered, 'And by thank you, I mean don't ever do that again. This isn't after-dinner theatre.'

'You might want to put your high beams on.' Ginger at least wanted to be able to see if there was a cattle grid up ahead; her spine, and teeth, would welcome the warning. But to be fair, Joyce wasn't actually driving at any great speed.

'Don't worry, I'll get you and your delicate anatomy home in one piece. Apart from anything, I want to make sure you're in a fit state for whatever we get up to next weekend. If this is a sign of things to come, then life around you will never be boring. Just swear to me, you'll get a more supportive bra. This will be the last time you experience me modifying my driving, and I'm only doing it out of sympathy – something I'm not renowned for.'

Her voice was severe, but she reached over and gave Ginger's hand a squeeze.

'Nightcap?' she offered.

'Definitely, maybe more than one.' There was a brief pause before Ginger spoke again. 'I was thinking, I could do with a break after all this. If I promise there won't be a murder involved, do you fancy a girls' weekend away?'

'Sounds right up my alley. And if there is another murder… well, I reckon you and I will put our heads together and figure it out.'

'Marvellous.' Ginger clapped her hands together. 'I'll put my thinking cap on, come up with somewhere fun for us to go.'

Joyce put her foot down and shot over a cattle grid. Ginger bit her tongue and yelped in pain. She'd changed her mind; there might very well be another murder.

If you enjoyed *Tales from Charleton House* sign up to Kate P Adams' newsletter at www.katepadams.com to find out when the next in the series is available to buy, and get a free Charleton House Mystery.

I HOPE YOU ENJOYED THIS BOOK

I really hope you enjoyed reading this book as much as I did writing it. I would love you more than I love coffee, gin and chocolate brownies if you could go on to Amazon and leave a review right this very moment. Even if it's just a one sentence comment, your words make a massive difference.

Amazon reviews are a huge boost to independently published authors like me who don't have big publishing houses to spread the word for us. The more reviews, the more likely it is that this book will be discovered by other readers.

Thank you so much
Kate

READ A FREE CHARLETON HOUSE MYSTERY

Building a relationship with my readers is one of the best things about writing. I occasionally send newsletters with details on new releases, special offers, interviews and articles relating to The Charleton House Mysteries.

Sign up to my mailing list and you'll also receive the very first Charleton House Mystery, *A Stately Murder*.

Head to my website for your free copy and find out what happens when Sophie stumbles across the victim of the first murder Charleton House has ever known.

www.katepadams.com

ABOUT THE AUTHOR

After 25 years working in some of England's finest buildings, Kate P. Adams has turned to murder.

Kate grew up in Derbyshire, the setting for the Charleton House Mysteries, and went on to work in theatres around the country, the Natural History Museum - London, the University of Oxford and Hampton Court Palace. Every day she explored darkened corridors and rooms full of history behind doors the public never get to enter. Kate spent years in these beautiful buildings listening to fantastic tales, wondering where the bodies were hidden, and hoping that she'd run into a ghost or two.

Kate has an unhealthy obsession with finding the perfect cup of coffee, enjoys a gin and tonic, and is managed by Pumpkin, a domineering tabby cat who is a little on the large side. Now that she lives in the USA, writing the Charleton House Mysteries allows Kate to go home to her beloved Derbyshire everyday, in her head at least.

ACKNOWLEDGEMENTS

Many thanks to my advance readers; your support and feedback means a great deal to me.

I'm extremely grateful to Richard Mason, my police advisor who guides me on procedure and makes sure I am, largely, within the law. When I break the rules, that's all me!

My talented editor Alison Jack, and Julia Gibbs, my eagle-eyed proofreader. It is an education and a pleasure to work with them.

Made in the USA
Middletown, DE
30 December 2021

57269294R00078